I0620840

THE SPIRIT OF LOVE

Barbara Cartland

Barbara Cartland Ebooks Ltd

This edition © 2020

ISBNs

9781788673013   EPUB

9781788673020   PAPERBACK

Book design by M-Y Books
m-ybooks.co.uk

THE BARBARA CARTLAND ETERNAL COLLECTION

The Barbara Cartland Eternal Collection is the unique opportunity to collect all five hundred of the timeless beautiful romantic novels written by the world's most celebrated and enduring romantic author.

Named the Eternal Collection because Barbara's inspiring stories of pure love, just the same as love itself, the books will be published on the internet at the rate of four titles per month until all five hundred are available.

The Eternal Collection, classic pure romance available worldwide for all time .

THE LATE DAME BARBARA CARTLAND

Barbara Cartland, who sadly died in May 2000 at the grand age of ninety eight, remains one of the world's most famous romantic novelists. With worldwide sales of over one billion, her outstanding 723 books have been translated into thirty six different languages, to be enjoyed by readers of romance globally.

Writing her first book 'Jigsaw' at the age of 21, Barbara became an immediate bestseller. Building upon this initial success, she wrote continuously throughout her life, producing bestsellers for an astonishing 76 years. In addition to Barbara Cartland's legion of fans in the UK and across Europe, her books have always been immensely popular in the USA. In 1976 she achieved the unprecedented feat of having books at numbers 1 & 2 in the prestigious B. Dalton Bookseller bestsellers list.

Although she is often referred to as the 'Queen of Romance', Barbara Cartland also wrote several historical biographies, six autobiographies and numerous theatrical plays as well as books on life, love, health and cookery. Becoming one of Britain's most popular media personalities and dressed in her trademark pink, Barbara spoke on radio and television about social and political issues, as well as making many public appearances.

In 1991 she became a Dame of the Order of the British Empire for her contribution to literature and her work for humanitarian and charitable causes.

Known for her glamour, style, and vitality Barbara Cartland became a legend in her own lifetime. Best remembered for her wonderful romantic novels and loved by millions of readers worldwide, her books remain treasured for their heroic heroes, plucky heroines and traditional values. But above all, it was Barbara Cartland's overriding belief in the positive power of love to help, heal and improve the quality of life for everyone that made her truly unique.

AUTHOR'S NOTE

This is the five hundredth book I have written and I have chosen for it my favourite period – the Regency.

I owe dozens of plots for my books to my dear friend, the late Sir Arthur Bryant. He used to laugh when I told him that I plagiarised his brilliant books and said that he was delighted for me to do so.

I owe so much to his books *The Years of Endurance 1773-1802*, *The Years of Victory 1802-1812* and *The Age of Elegance 1812-1822*.

When Sir Arthur gave me his last book, *The Spirit of England*, he inscribed it,

'To Barbara who understands so well.

With the affection and admiration of the Author.

I must therefore dedicate this, my five hundredth book, *THE SPIRIT OF LOVE*

To Sir Arthur Bryant

One of our greatest historians whose books, fascinating, human and inspiring, will live forever in the hearts

Of those who love ENGLAND.

CHAPTER ONE
1814

As the open carriage turned into a road where a great number of people were moving about, there was the sound of music in the distance.

Odella Wayne, who was sitting on the back seat, bent forward to see if she could discern where this delightful music was coming from.

When she could see what was happening and that people were moving hastily to clear the road, she gave an exclamation.

"It's the circus!"

The maid, who was sitting opposite her, then exclaimed,

"Miss Odella, how ever so excitin'!"

The coachman, an elderly man who had been driving the Rector for many years, pulled the horse to one side.

"We'll 'ave to wait 'ere, Miss Odella," he said over his shoulder, "till they passes by."

"That is a good idea, Thompson," Odella replied, "and it will give us an excellent view of them as they go past us."

She realised that Emily, the maid, was straining to see what she could over her shoulder.

"Come and sit beside me, Emily," she suggested kindly. "You will have a much better view from this seat."

"Oh, thank you, Miss Odella," Emily answered. "I've always been mad about the circus ever since I were a child."

Odella smiled, knowing that it was not so many years ago.

When she had made up her mind, since her father was away from home, to go shopping in Portsmouth, she had ordered the carriage that he usually travelled in.

She suggested to the housekeeper, Mrs. Barnet, that she should come with her, but the elderly woman replied,

"I 'ave to refuse, Miss Odella. I've got too much on me 'ands to do. When the Master's away, it's me one chance of gettin' 'is study really well cleaned. You know 'ow he goes on if we disturb 'is books when 'e's at 'ome."

Odella smiled.

"I am sure you are right to take the opportunity," she agreed. "Papa does get very upset if we move his books, especially those he is using for his research."

The Rector was writing a history of the village of Nettleway, which was his Parish.

As he required a great many books for reference, they were piled up on every table in the study and on the floor as well.

She could easily understand Mrs. Barnet's desire to make everything clean while she had a good chance.

"There are some things I want to buy in Portsmouth," Odella said, "so I will take Emily with me. I know Papa would not like me to go there alone."

"I should think not indeed!" Mrs. Barnet declared as if Odella had suggested something improper. "And your dear mother, God rest her soul, would never have let you go into the town on your own."

That was certainly true because Portsmouth at the moment was very different from the Portsmouth of old before the war.

Now that the tide seemed to have turned against Napoleon Bonaparte and every day the Duke of Wellington was sending home most encouraging reports of progress on all fronts and so people were very much more cheerful than they had been the previous year.

And last spring and summer the roads to Portsmouth and Plymouth had been filled with troops.

There were the jangling Household Cavalry with splendid accoutrements on excellent horses who were to travel with them to their destination.

There were Reserve Battalions marching to reinforce their Regiments, who were by now veterans of the Peninsular War and several detachments of rosy-cheeked Militiamen under raw young Ensigns 'in fine new toggery'.

They came through the villages, their drums and fifes playing, with little boys running excitedly behind them.

The housewives rushed to their cottage doors and windows to see them passing and the older women mourned over the 'young lambs going to the slaughter'.

The older men and those who had returned wounded to England muttered that they did not know what was 'a-comin' to 'em'.

Odella and her father often talked of the carnage awaiting them after they had crossed the English Channel and she wondered what the soldiers would think when they saw the barren tawny shores of the Peninsula for the first time.

The men who returned would come to tell the Rector of their experiences, feeling that he was the one person in the village who would understand all that they had been through.

They would describe all too vividly and in detail the stink of Lisbon and what they felt as they marched out of the Belem Barracks on the long mountain track to the frontier between Portugal and Spain.

Some of the stories they told had made Odella want to cry, but others were very funny.

One young man who had returned home only slightly wounded was the doctor's son, Tim Howland.

He described vividly to the Rector, whom he had known since he was a child, what he and the men with him had experienced.

Bug-bitten, footsore and dusty, they had finally found themselves among the tattered cheery veterans who were to be their comrades.

"It was then that our education began," Tim related.

The Rector raised his eyebrows and he went on to explain,

"I and a large number of others were taken by Major O'Hara of the Rifles to where we could look down from a rocky height at the enemy on the plain below.

"'Those are the French,' he barked out in his Barrack yard voice. 'You must kill those fellows and not allow them to kill you. You must learn to do as these old birds do and find cover where you can. Remember, recruits, you have come here to kill, not to be killed. Bear this in mind – if you don't kill the French first, they will kill you!'"

"That was certainly plain-speaking," the Rector remarked.

"That is what we thought at the time," Tim replied. "And it was true enough, as we were to find out for ourselves."

After what she had heard, Odella had then always prayed for each consignment of men as they arrived.

Marching behind the drums and fifes, the soldiers obviously were enjoying the cheers of the crowd.

They appreciated the young girls who ran out to thrust flowers into their hands or give them kisses and she wondered how many would return and how many would be buried in unmarked graves.

At the beginning of his great offensive in May 1813, the Duke of Wellington had under his command more than fifty thousand British troops and nearly thirty thousand Portuguese.

Now, by the following February, Wellington had a firm foothold across the Pyrenees in the South-West of France and the people of Spain had become our friends and allies.

"Oh, miss, oh, do look!" Emily cried.

As the music grew louder, it was certainly not the fifes and drums that Odella had heard so often.

Now she leant over her side of the carriage to look up the road and she was not surprised that Emily was feeling so enthusiastic.

There was a colourful parade coming down the street towards them.

It was led by a tall man wearing a red coat and black top hat, which he raised every so often to the women waving to him.

He was riding a fine black horse and behind him there were four other horses ridden by pretty young women wearing ballet skirts that revealed their shapely legs.

On their heads they wore glittering crowns and fluttering feathers and what looked like flashing jewels.

Emily was so thrilled that she rose off the seat beside Odella and then, kneeling on the opposite seat, which had its back to the horses, she could see better without obscuring her Mistress's view.

Nearer and nearer they came.

Now Odella could see that the band was being carried on a wagon drawn by two white horses and they were driven by a man wearing the skin and head of a tiger.

Cymbals were clashed to make the loudest noise possible and the big drum boomed out to the delight of the crowd.

The bandsmen were all dressed in fairy costumes.

This wagon was followed by some clowns who cracked jokes with the passers-by and waved balloons on sticks in front of the children. They whisked them away, however, before the boys could catch them.

With their white faces, exaggerated red lips, and strange pantaloons, it was impossible not to laugh at them.

Every movement they made and every word they uttered brought peals of laughter from those they were passing.

On another wagon covered not like the others in scarlet but in glittering silver, came a spectacular figure.

Seated on what appeared to be a golden Throne, she was dressed in a shimmering gown that caught the sun's rays and glittered with every movement she made.

It covered not only her body but also her head and she wore over her face what Odella recognised as a *yashmak*.

Her eyes were revealed, but beneath them there was a veil of rose-pink gauze.

In one hand she held a large crystal ball and in the other a pack of cards.

"She be the fortune-teller, Miss Odella!" Emily gasped. "I've 'eard about 'er."

Odella thought that she certainly looked the part.

Then, just as they reached a point on the road where they were watching from, the man in the red coat called a halt.

He drew in his horse, as did those behind him, and the two wagons came to a standstill.

"Ladies and Gentlemen!" he called out in a voice that seemed to echo round the houses and hushed the crowds into silence. "Friends of Portsmouth. This afternoon at three o'clock there will be a performance of the circus in Lincoln Field and another at six. Come and join us! Come and see the brilliance of our ballerinas on horseback and the way that our clowns can make you laugh and consult Madame Zosina, who will tell you what wonderful surprises await you in the future."

He paused for a moment to say even more impressively,

"Because we all wish 'good luck' to the brave men fighting for us against Napoleon, Madame Zosina will tell the future of every Serviceman for half the price that she charges to the rest of us."

There were loud cheers at this.

Madame Zosina bent her head in acknowledgement, first to one side of the street and then to the other.

"Three o'clock!" the Ringmaster shouted out. "And don't be late!"

Then the band struck up a bright tune and they were off again with the people waving to them on the pavements and from the windows.

They were accompanied by a crowd of small boys running excitedly beside the horses and the wagons.

As they disappeared round a corner of the street, Emily gave a deep sigh,

"That were lovely, Miss Odella, I'd love to 'ave me fortune told."

She looked pleadingly at Odella as she spoke.

Because Odella was fond of the girl, who was only just seventeen and a year younger than herself, she replied,

"If we can complete our shopping quickly, perhaps we can then go to the circus."

Emily clasped her hands together.

"Oh, Miss Odella, do you mean that? It'll be somethin' I'll remember all me life!"

"I hope you will have a great deal more than that to remember," Odella remarked. "As we don't have to hurry home to give my father his tea, we will go to the circus, but we must finish our shopping first."

The carriage was already moving and Thompson turned at the far end of the street.

Odella had made a list of the things that were wanted both by Mrs. Barnet, who was short of cleaning materials, and by Betsy the cook.

Betsy had been at the Rectory for many years and was always complaining that the local shops did not stock the special ingredients she wanted for more exotic dishes.

It was an old complaint that Odella had heard a hundred times before.

She had therefore brought with her now a list of exactly what Betsy really wanted.

Although it took time, they managed to purchase almost everything they required before it was a quarter to three.

Odella was aware that, while she was asking for first one thing and then another, Emily was steadfastly watching the clock.

She was desperately afraid that, if they were late, they would not be able to obtain seats in the ring of the circus.

Odella thought, however, that it was most unlikely that the circus would be full up in the afternoon.

It was in the evening, when the shops were closed and people had nothing else to do, that they would flock to Lincoln Field, where the circus had been set up. And then every seat would be taken.

When finally Odella told Thompson where to take them, Emily was almost jumping for joy.

"Now, what do you want to do, Emily?" Odella asked her. "Shall we go into the Big Top and watch the clowns and the horses, and I expect there will be monkeys too, or do you want to visit Madame Zosina first?"

Emily thought it over and, as she was not very quick-witted, it took her some time.

"I thinks, Miss Odella," she replied at last, "we should go to Madame Zosina first. There won't be many people waitin' to see her early in the afternoon and later 'er might leave afore we gets to 'er."

Odella laughed, thinking that this was good reasoning on Emily's part.

"Very well," she smiled, "It is Madame Zosina first."

When they arrived at Lincoln Field, it was easy to see Madame's tent.

It stood away from the others by itself and instead of being like the other tents, it was red with her name emblazoned on it in gold lettering. And outside the tent there were two large palm trees each standing in a tub.

Odella purchased their tickets at a booth and she and Emily went inside.

There was a row of chairs on either side of the tent entrance for those who were waiting to go into the inner sanctum.

Madame Zosina was hidden from their gaze by a glittering curtain rather like the gown she wore and the veil that covered her hair.

Odella realised how everything was designed to excite the imagination and anticipation of those who consulted the famous fortune-teller.

There were two sailors waiting to have their fortunes told and, almost as soon as Odella and Emily had sat down, another sailor came out through the glittering curtain.

He went up to those who were waiting and as the nearest one jumped up to take his place behind the curtain, he said to him,

"She be marvellous! That's what she be. And you'll be proud to know me afore I'm very much older!"

The man he was speaking to then disappeared through the glittering curtain.

His friend, who was left behind, laughed.

"If she's told you you're goin' to be an Admiral, well, you just shouldn't believe all you hears!"

"You'll be surprised," the other young sailor retorted.

Then he walked jauntily out of the tent into the sunshine and the sailor he had just been talking to moved up nearer to the curtain.

In case someone came and tried to steal a march on them, Odella moved into the seat next to him and Emily rapidly came up beside her.

They had only just done so when three girls came into the tent and hastily took chairs on the other side.

"We're goin' to have to wait," one of the girls whispered.

"'T'll be worth it to know the future," another girl replied. "I wants to know if Bert's serious or not. He talks an awful lot, but he don't say what I wants to hear."

Odella smiled to herself.

She reflected that it was not very difficult to tell the fortunes of the village girls, which was something that she had quite often done herself.

Ever since she had been a child, she had somehow known things about people without being told.

She had been a fortune-teller for her father at the Bazaar they held every summer for the Church and again when they wanted to raise money for the many festivities at Christmas.

The village people thought that she was brilliant at her fortune-telling and believed every _word she told them.

Her mother had warned her always to be very careful and not raise people's false hopes.

"I know, darling, that you sometimes see things that other people cannot see and that is a gift direct from God. But you must not abuse it. You must not promise things that cannot be fulfilled for people who do not acquire what they are wishing for as it can make them very unhappy."

Odella had understood her mother implicitly.

She had therefore always been very ambiguous in her fortune-telling.

Unless she was absolutely convinced that what she said would actually happen, she did not raise the person's hopes.

It had been difficult for her since the scale of the war had increased.

Almost every cottage in the village had someone fighting on the Peninsula against the French.

Although she had never revealed it to anyone, she had somehow been fully aware of the deaths of several young men. And long before their relatives had been informed, Odella knew that they had died in the service of their country.

But she had on two occasions been quite certain that a man would return back to his home after his family had finally given him up for lost.

She had been proved right when one of the men had arrived back wounded and the other had been blinded by cannon fire.

She thought now that it would be interesting to see exactly how Madame Zosina treated her clients.

She wanted to find out as well if she was a genuine fortune-teller or only someone acting the part.

It was usual when any circus visited the towns of Portsmouth or Gosport that there would be a fortune-teller among the entertainers.

But from all she had heard, Odella was certain that most of them were not genuine and they merely preyed on the human frailty of people wanting to know the future before it had actually happened.

The second sailor seemed to be with Madame Zosina for quite a long time.

When he came out through the curtain, he was beaming.

"You 'ave a go, Joe," he said to his friend. "I'll wait for you outside."

As he went out smiling, Joe went through the glittering curtain and Odella moved up yet another seat.

Now she could hear faintly, but none the less clearly what was being said inside the tent.

"Good day, sailor," a soft voice greeted him.

"G'day, ma'am," the sailor replied. "Me friends 'ave bin tellin' me 'ow good you be and so I wants to 'ear what's goin' to 'appen to me."

"I expect you are going abroad," Madame Zosina said again very softly. "You are eager to know what will happen to you when you reach your destination."

"That be right," Joe agreed.

There was silence.

Odella guessed that, as he sat in front of her, Madame Zosina was gazing into her crystal ball.

She was proved right, when after a few seconds Madame carried on,

"I see you travelling in a big ship and I think you are going to France."

Joe must have nodded an affirmative and she continued,

"You have to say 'goodbye' to a lovely young lady."

"That's right," Joe confirmed. "Will she be faithful to me while I'm away?"

"I just know she will be," Zosina replied, "but I think you are feeling unhappy at leaving her."

Joe murmured something that Odella could not hear and Madame Zosina went on,

"You have not very long to tell her how much you love her. You are leaving sooner than you expected."

There was silence before she added,

"Now, let me see – is it three days or four before you sail?"

"'Tis three," Joe said eagerly.

"Then you must tell her tonight that you love her and every night until you go. And now let me look into my crystal ball, your ship is very large, if I can make out its name, I will give you a special talisman to keep you safe wherever you are going."

"Thank you, ma'am. I'd like that ever so much."

"It is, in fact, very very lucky," Zosina said, "but I must first find the name of your ship."

There was silence until Joe admitted,

"We be told to tell no one the name of our ship."

"I can understand that," Zosina said quickly. "But I see it clearly in my crystal ball. Now, let me think – "

She must, Odella thought, be peering into her crystal ball again.

After a minute she murmured,

"I see an '*L*' or is it an '*I*'?"

"An '*I*'," Joe said quickly.

"Now I see another letter that looks to me like an '*M*'."

"That be an '*N*'," Joe volunteered.

"Am I wrong or is the word *INVINCIBLE*?" Madame Zosina asked.

"You be right," Joe said, "and that be real clever of you."

"Very well. Here is your talisman and next Wednesday, or is it Thursday, you sail?"

"I thinks it be Wednesday night, ma'am."

"Then on Wednesday I will think of you and make sure you arrive at your destination safely."

"Thank you, thank you very much," Joe enthused.

"I will make sure too that your girl thinks of you," Madame said. "It's important that she should not forget you while you are away."

"I be grateful, very grateful, ma'am."

There was the rattling sound of a chair being pushed back and then Joe came through the curtains.

As he did so, Odella realised that a man wearing a soldier's uniform was standing beside her.

"Could I ask you," he said, "if you'd let me go in to see the fortune-teller before you? We've been told to be back in Barracks by four o'clock and I just dare not be late."

"Yes, of course," Odella agreed. "I am in no hurry."

"Thank you very much."

The soldier disappeared through the glittering curtain.

Listening again, Odella heard Madame Zosina talk to him in very much the same soft gentle way that she had talked to Joe.

She managed at the same time to extract from him the information that he was leaving the day after tomorrow just as she had done with Joe.

She found out the name of his ship and also the Regiments that were sailing with him.

It was so cleverly done that Odella could hardly believe what she was hearing.

Yet, without his realising it, she had made the soldier tell her everything she wanted to know.

As Odella felt the horror of what was happening, she thought that it could not be true.

There had been talk throughout the war about spies who had been able to infiltrate into England with the smugglers.

Men and women had been bribed into betraying secrets that would be of considerable use to Napoleon.

Her father had said often enough that it was dangerous to chatter to strangers, however innocent they might appear.

"Because we live near Portsmouth," he had told Odella, "we have to be more careful than anyone else. Just one careless word could alert the enemy that a ship is leaving from here. Then the French are waiting to attack it as soon as it puts out to sea."

It had, however, never occurred to Odella that men who were sworn to secrecy could be beguiled into revealing information to sinister women like Madame Zosina.

Their unguarded words had resulted in their ships being sunk and many lives being lost.

Now she heard Madame Zosina giving the soldier some sort of talisman and assuring him that through her magic powers he would be safe wherever he was going.

Odella wanted to scream out that the woman was a spy and a danger to our armed forces at war.

Then she knew that she would have to be very careful and discreet about what she had heard.

She was quite certain that, if Madame Zosina became aware that anyone was suspicious of her, she would quickly disappear or else take some evasive action that could turn out to be extremely unpleasant for anyone who denounced her.

When the soldier reappeared through the curtain, Odella told Emily to go in first.

"Oh, no, Miss Odella. 'Tis your turn next," Emily insisted.

"I have a headache," Odella then told her. "You go in and, if it is still bad, I can come back another day."

"I'm real sorry, Miss Odella," Emily said.

However, she quickly hurried past her to where Madame Zosina was waiting.

Listening to what was being said, Odella was aware that it was very different from what she had listened to before.

Emily was promised that a tall handsome man would fall in love with her before the end of the year.

But she would have to be very careful about another man who was unpleasant and should be avoided or he would make plenty of trouble for her.

"You will receive a message from overseas that will please you," Madame Zosina went on.

"That'll be me brother," Emily answered quickly.

"I think you will be seeing him sooner than you expect," the fortune-teller finished.

"Well, that be good news, very good news!" Emily replied.

When she came out, she was beaming at what she had just heard.

But to her surprise, Odella hurried her out of the tent and into the sunshine.

"I must go home," she said.

"Be your 'ead very bad, Miss Odella?" Emily asked. "P'raps Madame Zosina could have done somethin' for you. Her's magic, she really is!"

"I am sure she is," Odella nodded.

They then walked across the field to where Thompson had parked the carriage under the shade of a lime tree.

As they climbed into it, Odella had an idea.

"I have to see the Lord Lieutenant, the Earl of Portsmouth," she said. "We will call there on our way home."

"Very good, Miss Odella," Thompson replied, "but it be a mile or so out of our way."

"There is no hurry and I am sure that his Lordship will not keep me long."

Thompson drove the carriage slowly over the rough ground and out onto the road where there were a number of people making their way to the Big Top.

"Oh, Miss Odella, we be missin' the circus!" Emily wailed.

"Perhaps we will be able to come again before the end of this week," Odella said. "I am sorry, Emily, but I don't want to sit in a hot stuffy tent at the moment."

"I understands, miss, but I did want to see them clowns."

"We will try and come tomorrow or perhaps the day after," Odella replied, "and after all, you have seen Madame Zosina now."

"She be magic!" Emily exclaimed. 'There be no other word for it, Miss Odella, real *magic*!"

Odella did not reply.

She was thinking that Zosina's magic was dangerous, very dangerous indeed.

And the sooner she did something about it the better.

CHAPTER TWO

The Marquis of Midhurst drove down Piccadilly, fully aware that all the passers-by were staring at his horses.

He was feeling particularly proud of the pair he was driving now which he had bought two weeks previously at Tattersalls Salesrooms.

He was really astonished when he had first seen them because he could not imagine that anyone who possessed such magnificent horseflesh would be willing to part with them.

When he learned that their owner had died, he then understood.

They had come from the North and there were a number of other active bidders when the sale started.

However they were eventually knocked down to the Marquis and he was delighted to be the possessor of them.

He found that they had been extremely well trained in addition to their obvious beauty.

When they were attached to his new phaeton, which was yellow with black wheels and shafts, he knew that they made a spectacle that was outstanding.

He turned down St. James's Street and hoped that some of his friends would see him pass from the window of White's Club.

He thought that after he had seen the Prime Minister he would go back to the Club and hear their comments on his new acquisition.

What had given him particular pleasure when he had inherited his father's title and vast estates was that he could now buy spirited horses that would always outpace any others on the Racecourse.

It went without saying that he was himself an outstanding rider and had been victorious in a number of arduous Steeplechases.

But there is always a penalty for everything.

He had on his father's death to leave the Army and this had taken away some of the glitter from the sublime possessions that he had inherited.

He had been wounded in Spain while serving with the Duke of Wellington's Army and sent back to England to recover.

As he reached Portsmouth despite Napoleon's ships, which were out to sink everything that moved in the Bay of Biscay, the third Marquis of Midhurst died.

His son was then informed that he must not re-join his Regiment.

The Senior Officers at the War Office and the Prince Regent himself explained that, if a Nobleman of his high standing was taken prisoner or killed, it would be a major triumph for Napoleon Bonaparte, who was definitely in need of considerable success in his constant war against all of Europe.

The Marquis had been angry because he enjoyed being a soldier. He loved his Regiment and had already received two awards for gallantry.

He knew, however, that the Senior Officers and the Prince Regent were talking sense.

Therefore he said to himself that it was no use 'kicking against the pricks'.

'Perhaps I can serve my country in some other way,' he pondered.

So far, however, he had not been asked to do anything concrete and instead concentrated on enjoying himself.

This was not in any way difficult, considering that he was very handsome, besides being of social consequence and extremely rich.

There was not a woman in all of London who did not dream of attracting the Marquis's attention and every woman certainly made every effort to do so.

In fact, as one of the Marquis's contemporaries moaned,

"The trouble with you, Midhurst, is that as soon as you enter a room, the tempo rises. How can we poor 'also rans' possibly compete with that?"

The Marquis chuckled.

At the same time he was well aware that he had a wide field to choose from in London.

He would have been inhuman if he had not enjoyed picking out the prettiest and most attractive women who fluttered their eyelashes at him.

He was very involved at the moment with one of the most exciting women he had ever met.

Lady Georgina Langford was a recognised beauty at twenty-seven and had been the toast of St. James's for several years. She did not seem likely to relinquish her leading role and the fact that she was known as 'the Tigress' was certainly justified.

The Marquis, with all his experience of women, had indeed never met a woman more passionate or more insatiable.

Lady Georgina had eloped when she was only eighteen with Walter Langford, who had little to recommend him except a handsome face.

He was known in all the Clubs as an inveterate gambler and he had pursued a number of women before he persuaded the Duke of Cumbria's daughter to run away with him.

The Duke was predictably furious.

Lady Georgina had been married to Walter Langford at the Mayfair Chapel, where the Parson asked no questions and required no credentials from those he married.

The Ceremony was nevertheless legal and so there was nothing that the Duke could do. And Walter most definitely enjoyed being his son-in-law.

His Grace, however, held very tightly onto the purse strings as might have been expected under the circumstances.

Walter Langford therefore made no trouble when his wife accepted expensive presents from her coterie of admirers.

There were jewels, furs, and other gifts that he could not possibly have afforded himself at any time.

To everybody's surprise the marriage seemed to be a happy one and there were no scenes or reproaches when Lady Georgina was engaged with her latest conquest.

There were fortunately no children of the marriage. The Langfords managed to live in a style that could never have been financed by Walter's success or lack of success at the card tables.

From the Marquis's present point of view, the fact that Walter was not jealous of him and Georgina was available when he required her made things very convenient.

He was thinking as he drove past St. James's Palace that he was to dine with her tonight and he also intended to take her a present of a delightfully pretty bracelet that he had seen in an expensive jeweller's window in Bond Street.

It would certainly embellish the whiteness of her hands with their long fingers and he smiled to himself as he thought of how she would thank him.

He had already learnt that Walter had gone to Newmarket for the races.

The Marquis turned his horses into Pall Mall and then he ceased to think about Georgina.

Instead he was wondering why the Prime Minister had asked to see him on a matter of some urgency.

He had met the second Earl of Liverpool before on various occasions, but had not been particularly impressed by him.

He had been born 'Robert Jenkinson' and had played a few minor parts in a number of Governments ever since he had grown up.

Equally his handling of the long war of attrition against Napoleon and the French had not been outstanding.

The Marquis, like many other people, thought wistfully of Pitt, who had died in 1806.

As he moved through Horseguards Parade towards Downing Street, he was thinking that, although the Prime Minister did his best, he was hardly in the class of those Prime Ministers who had made a real impression on the public and on the enemies of England.

Reaching Downing Street, he drew up his horses with a flourish outside Number 10 and handed the reins to his groom.

As the door was opened to him, he walked in, wondering once again why he had been sent for.

He was told that the Prime Minister was waiting for him in his sitting room.

As he was escorted there, the Marquis wondered if any man at any time had politically to face such problems as the Prime Minister of England at that particular moment in history.

The war had gone on year after year.

Now there was indeed a glimmer of hope that it might end before too long.

It required a very strong man to make sure politically that, if we did win the war, we did not lose the peace.

"The Most Honourable Marquis of Midhurst," the butler who was escorting the Marquis announced in a loud voice as he opened the door to the sitting room with a flourish.

As the Marquis walked in, he realised that the Prime Minister was not alone.

The Secretary of State for War, the Viscount Castlereagh, was with him.

He was an old friend and, when the Marquis had shaken hands first with the Prime Minister and then with the Viscount, he said,

"It is delightful, Castlereagh, to see you again."

"And I have been looking forward to seeing you," the Viscount replied. "Have you now recovered completely from your terrible wound?"

"I still limp a little, which really infuriates me, but, thank God, I can ride a horse and I still have two legs!"

The Prime Minister and the Viscount both laughed heartily and then they all sat down in comfortable armchairs placed near the fire.

"I have a message for you from Wellington, who has asked in his despatches how you are," the Viscount remarked. "He also told me to tell you that he misses you."

"And I miss him," the Marquis replied. "You will know that above all things, I wanted to return to my Regiment."

"We just cannot go into all that again!" the Prime Minister intervened quickly. "We have asked you here, Marquis, because we have a very tricky situation in your County."

The Marquis raised his eyebrows.

"In Hampshire?"

"Exactly," the Prime Minister replied. "And we thought that it was something that you could deal with your usual aplomb."

The Marquis was becoming more and more curious as to what it could possibly be.

The question that sprang to his mind was answered before it could reach his lips.

"Perhaps you are wondering why we have not already approached the Lord Lieutenant?" the Prime Minister said. "The answer is simply that the Earl of Portsmouth is an old man and has indicated that he wished to retire at the end of this year."

"I thought that was what he might do," the Marquis commented.

"And, of course," the Prime Minister went on, "you will take his place."

The Marquis, who had already assumed that this was as a foregone conclusion, merely nodded his head.

"Now the reason that we have asked you to come here," the Viscount said, "is that we are desperately worried about the ships that are leaving from Portsmouth Harbour."

The Marquis looked surprised.

"I know, of course, that there are a great number of them."

"We have now divided the troops we send out to Wellington between Portsmouth and Plymouth,"

Viscount Castlereagh explained, "but the many casualties from Portsmouth are continuing to give us a great deal of anxiety."

"Casualties?" the Marquis queried.

"The ships put to sea at night, as you know," the Viscount responded. "The troops board them at dusk and, when they reach the open sea, they wait until it is dark before they move any further."

The Marquis, who knew this, nodded his head.

"Every man aboard them," the Viscount went on, "is warned never to divulge to anyone the exact date and time of a ship's embarkation."

The Marquis was well aware of this and so he said nothing.

The Prime Minister spoke next,

"What Castlereagh is trying to say," he said, "is that for the last month the ships leaving Portsmouth have been attacked by French vessels that appear to be lying in wait for them as if they already knew the date and time they could expect them."

The Marquis drew in his breath.

"Are you telling me that there are spies in Portsmouth who are extracting information from the troops, which results in the French Navy knowing exactly when ships carrying them will leave the Harbour?"

"That is what I am trying to say," the Prime Minister agreed, "although it seems almost impossible."

"I suppose that nothing is impossible in war," the Marquis remarked. "But it is difficult to understand how the information obtained through careless talk can be carried so quickly across the Channel to the French Navy, what is left of it after the Battle of Trafalgar."

He spoke the last words scathingly and Viscount Castlereagh said rapidly,

"It would be a mistake, Midhurst, to underrate their intelligence, especially if it enables them to destroy our forces before they even have a chance of going into battle under the Duke of Wellington."

"I agree with you," the Marquis replied, "but what do you suggest should be done about it?"

"That is exactly why we have asked you to come here today," the Prime Minister said. "Portsmouth is in your County. Besides which, if there is any man who can cope with this particular situation, it is yourself."

"You flatter me," the Marquis replied.

At the same time he knew that he had on two separate occasions changed a defeat into a victory by being perceptively aware of what the enemy would do next.

"Wellington informed me," Viscount Castlereagh said, "that it was you who had advised him, before you were invalided home, that as soon as he crossed the Pyrenees into France he should foster goodwill with the civilian population."

The Marquis did not confirm this.

However, he had worked out that if the English were to retain numerical superiority in the field, they could spare no troops to hold down territory in the rear.

When the midwinter rains had bogged down the Armies, Wellington remembered the Marquis's advice about the local population.

He devoted himself to putting it into effect.

And in this he was actually helped by the French troops.

After enjoying twenty years of rape, pillage and arson in all the countries of Europe that they had overrun, they had recently behaved in the same way at home.

Most of the Spaniards had to be sent back to their homes because, as Wellington told their Commander, he had not sacrificed thousands of men to enable the survivors to rob the French.

The British troops included a large number of gaolbirds and these he treated in his usual realistic way by sending a strong force of Military Police up and down the columns.

They had orders to string up on the spot any man who was found pilfering and, after a few examples, there was no further plundering.

Such a manner of making war astonished the French and they could scarcely believe their eyes.

An innkeeper veteran of Napoleon's Italian campaigns was speechless when Brigadier Barnard of the Light Division asked him how much he owed for his dinner.

This policy, as the Prime Minister and Viscount Castlereagh well knew, had proved as valuable as a dozen victories.

The French in Southwestern France found themselves quartering an Army of gentlemen.

The British Commander-in-Chief even invited the Maires of the towns where he stayed to dine with him – a thing never heard of in a French Revolutionary General.

The result had been fantastic.

Those who had fled came flocking back to their homes and it was said that the British waged war only against men with arms in their hands.

What was more the British paid for all their requirements.

Before long the local inhabitants were coining money and fowls and turkeys were selling for large sums.

The Commissariat, instead of being starved of its supplies, was inundated with offers of cattle, grain, and fodder.

Almost as if the Viscount could read the Marquis's thoughts, he said,

"I learnt from the last despatch I have received that the French Bankers have offered the British cash and credit."

The Prime Minister laughed.

"I can tell you something more, an English Officer who is there wrote,

"*If this is what making war in an enemy country is like, I never wish to campaign in a friendly one again'*."

They all laughed and then the Prime Minister said,

"To be serious for a moment, Midhurst, if you were wise enough to give Wellington such brilliant advice in advance, I hope you can suggest how to save the men we are sending out to join Wellington from losing their lives at sea before they have even fired a shot."

"How many ships have been attacked so far?" the Marquis asked.

"Four," Lord Castlereagh replied. "The first one was sunk and nearly all those on board were drowned. The other three were well prepared for an attack and managed to drive off the enemy with, however, a number of casualties."

He sighed before he continued,

"As you can imagine, those in command at Portsmouth are extremely concerned about it. At the same time it is very hard to believe that information can be taken across to France so quickly."

"The smugglers don't take long to cross the Channel," the Prime Minister suggested.

"And I would suppose that nefarious trade is still flourishing!" the Marquis remarked sarcastically.

The Prime Minister made a helpless gesture with his hands.

"What can we do?" he asked. "Smugglers big and small operate at night on almost every inch of the South Coast. We have employed more Coastguards, provided them with faster ships and have a number of intelligence men trying to discover from which Harbours the smugglers leave."

"And the result?" the Marquis asked.

"I think perhaps we catch one in twenty," the Prime Minister replied gloomily.

"And as, of course, you are well aware," the Viscount added, "the goods they bring back to England are paid for in gold, which provides Napoleon with more arms and better guns to destroy our troops with."

"I have also heard," the Marquis said quietly, "that the smugglers bring back spies and even assassins. So, for God's sake, strengthen the guard on His Royal Highness. His death would be a tremendous moral victory for Bonaparte."

Both men stared at him in astonishment.

"How have you heard of that?" the Prime Minister asked.

"I have my ways of knowing things," the Marquis answered, "and I do beg of you to take care."

The Prime Minister sighed.

"There have been two attempts, which, to put it briefly, were nipped in the bud. But, of course, we are always vigilant."

"At this moment, when the tide is turning," the Marquis said, "your vigilance should be doubled. I can imagine nothing that would lower the morale of our brave men, who have now fought their way into France, more than to learn of a disaster of that sort."

"I promise you, Midhurst, we are doing our very best," the Prime Minister said, "but, as we have already said, the smugglers creep in and we cannot always know what they carry with them besides brandy and other contraband."

The Marquis thought that he sounded rather feeble and ineffective.

The increase in smuggling was a disgraceful state of affairs, he thought, but he did not say so.

Instead he addressed the Prime Minister,

"You have certainly presented me with a very tricky problem, but I will do my best to solve it. To be honest, however, I can think of no possible way that information about the movement of our ships, even if it is obtained from the men aboard them, can reach France even more quickly than the smugglers could carry it back."

"But the information does get there," the Viscount said, "and you have never yet been defeated in any undertaking."

"I hope that remains true," the Marquis replied, "but, as they say, there always has to be a first time –"

"I pray to God it is not this one," the Prime Minister finished.

They talked for a little while longer about the good news from the battlefront and then the Marquis left.

As he drove back the way he had come, he was thinking that never in his life had he been given a more difficult problem.

There must be a solution somewhere, of course there was.

But how was he to begin to find it? Where should he start?

The last question, of course, was answered easily. By leaving immediately for his house in Hampshire.

This was what he had to do and he recognised that it was his duty.

He must therefore apologise to Lady Georgina for not dining with her tonight as he had promised.

When he reached Piccadilly, he turned his horses up Berkeley Street and into Berkeley Square.

Lady Georgina and her husband had a very small house in Bruton Street. It was so small that it was overshadowed by the larger houses beside it.

The Marquis calculated that the rent could not be a very high one. At the same time they had a good address, which implied being in Mayfair.

As he drew up outside the front door, he took his gold watch from his waistcoat pocket and saw that it was after twelve o'clock.

There was always the possibility that Lady Georgina would have gone out to luncheon, in which case, he could only leave her a message.

He told his groom to get down from the box and ring the bell.

The door was briskly opened by an elderly servant and the Marquis was informed that her Ladyship had not yet come downstairs.

He then handed the reins to his groom and walked into the house.

He had, of course, been here often and the elderly servant, who had been tipped by him generously on various occasions, bowed obsequiously.

"It's nice to see your Lordship, but her Ladyship isn't expecting you."

"I am aware of that," the Marquis replied, "but please ask her Ladyship if she will see me at once as it is a matter of extreme urgency."

He walked into the small sitting room just off the hall.

The old servant hurried up the stairs as fast as his arthritic legs would carry him.

The Marquis walked to the window and looked out at the small garden that lay at the back of the house. It was used by quite a number of the adjacent house owners.

He was, however, not seeing the green grass or the flowerbeds filled with colour.

He was thinking about all those British ships, carrying no lights, but being attacked in the darkness because the enemy had learnt of their whereabouts.

He was very deep in his thoughts that he started when he heard Lady Georgina's voice behind him exclaim,

"It is really you! I was not expecting such an early visit."

"I know, but I had to see you," the Marquis replied.

She closed the door and walked towards him.

With the sunshine on her face, he was thinking how beautiful she was.

Her hair was dark, almost black, and yet it had strange lights in it that were picked out by the sunshine and her eyes were the dark blue of the Mediterranean.

She had told him laughingly that this was due to her Irish blood, which came from her mother,

"They always say that their blue eyes were put in with dirty fingers."

Hers certainly were framed by her long dark eyelashes through which she looked at him provocatively in a way that was irresistible.

As she reached him now, the Marquis's arms went out towards her.

She lifted her face.

He kissed her fiercely, feeling the fire on her lips as he touched them.

Her body seemed almost to melt into his.

Only when he raised his head did she insist,

"What has happened? Why are you here?"

"I have to go to the country," the Marquis explained, "so it is impossible for us to dine together tonight ."

"Oh, Dearest Michael, how can you think of deserting me when Walter is away and we can be together the whole night?"

"I do know," the Marquis sighed, "but unfortunately I have to go home. Something has happened that requires my personal attention immediately and which cannot possibly wait until tomorrow."

"Are you – quite sure of that?" Lady Georgina asked in a low seductive voice.

Then her lips were on his and her arms were round his neck.

He knew that she was pleading with him in a way that there was no need for words.

Only when they were both breathless did the Marquis, with a superhuman effort, put her to one side.

"You must forgive me, Georgina," he said in a deep voice, "but I have to leave you. It will not be for long."

"Let me come with you," Lady Georgina suggested.

Her eyes were looking up into his.

He could see the fire in them and knew only too well why she was talked of as being a tigress.

She was coaxing him with every breath she drew and with every movement of her body against his and with her lips that were inviting his kisses.

He looked at her for a moment before he said,

"I am so sorry, my dear, but it is a question of duty."

"Duty – to whom?" she asked and there was a sharp note in her voice.

"To myself," the Marquis replied.

He kissed her forehead lightly before he said,

"I meant to buy you, before we met for dinner tonight, a bracelet I saw in Bond Street and that I knew you would like. You shall have it immediately after I return and the earrings to go with it."

"Oh, Michael, you are so good to me!" Lady Georgina cried. "Even so, while I adore your presents, it is *you* I want."

"As I want you," the Marquis replied, "but now I must go."

He put her to one side as he spoke and walked towards the door.

He had almost reached it before she came running after him.

Flinging her arms around him once again and pulling his head down to hers, she sighed,

"I love you, Michael, and don't forget it while you are attending to anything so boring as your duty."

"I will be back as quickly as I can," the Marquis promised.

Once again he set her on one side and, although she tried to prevent him, he opened the door.

"Take good care of yourself," he said with a smile.

Then he was gone.

Only when she heard his footsteps moving across the hall and heard him speaking to a servant did Lady Georgina realise that she was defeated.

Angrily she stamped her foot.

How was it possible that anything called 'duty' could be more important than she was?

Then she remembered the bracelet and the earrings that the Marquis had promised her.

She told herself that, if he was away for too long, he would have to produce as well the necklace that went with them.

She knew how lovely it would look around her long white neck.

Going to the mirror over the mantelpiece, she looked in it, imagining how the jewels would enhance her beauty.

CHAPTER THREE

The Lord Lieutenant's house was an old one which had been added to over the centuries and it was set in a large garden and approached through a Park where there were a number of ancient oak trees and a small herd of deer.

Odella knew it well. The Earl of Portsmouth was a friend of her father's and she had often been taken to parties in the house with the Earl's grandchildren.

She thought now, as they drove up the long drive, that as Lord Lieutenant he would be the best person to advise her.

He would know exactly what she should do and who she should report to on what she had discovered.

She did not, however, want to upset him, as she had heard that he had been in ill health lately and was growing very old.

But she could think of no one else who she could go to at that particular moment.

And every nerve in her body told her that time was important.

If she shirked responsibility or delayed in any way getting the information to the right place, many more Englishmen would die.

Thompson then brought the carriage to a standstill outside the front door.

Without waiting Odella jumped out and ran up the steps to ring the doorbell.

There was a little wait before the door opened.

The elderly butler whom she had known since she was a child stood there in front of her.

"Why, it's Miss Odella!" he exclaimed in surprise.

"Yes, Hodgson, and I must speak to his Lordship as a matter of urgency."

"The Master's has someone with him at the moment," Hodgson informed her.

"It is really very important or I would not be bothering him," Odella replied.

"Then you had better go into the morning room, Miss Odella," the butler said after a moment's hesitation, "and I'll see what I can do."

"Thank you," Odella said with relief, "and I promise you I would not bother his Lordship if it was not something very urgent."

She did not wait for Hodgson to open the door, but let herself into the morning room, which overlooked the Park in front of the house.

It was a rather dull room and she thought that, when the Earl's eldest son inherited, he would have a great many repairs and renewals to attend to in the house.

Because she was so agitated, she could not sit still for a single minute.

She walked to the window to look out with unseeing eyes at the sun shining on the trees in the Park.

How was it possible, she wondered, that there were people in England who would betray the men who were fighting for freedom and their beloved country.

She thought how fervently her father prayed that the Duke of Wellington's Army might be victorious.

The news was indeed much better than it had been for some time and that made it seem incredible that our men were going to their deaths, not fighting the enemy, but simply while sailing from one Port to another.

'Something must be done about it,' Odella murmured to herself.

The door then opened and she thought that it was Hodgson returning to say that the Earl would see her.

To her surprise it was the Earl himself.

He came into the room, leaning heavily on a stick and it was obvious that it was an effort for him to walk.

"Hodgson tells me you want to see me urgently, my child," he said as Odella ran towards him.

"I had to come here and see you and, although I do know that you are very busy, this is something desperately important."

'Then let's sit down while you tell me all about it," the old man suggested kindly.

He seated himself in a high-backed chair in front of the fireplace.

Because she knew that he was rather deaf, Odella went down on her knees beside his chair.

"I have just come from Portsmouth," she began, "and although it is – hard to believe – I discovered – a spy there!"

"A pie?" the Earl asked with a puzzled expression on his face.

"A *spy*!" Odella repeated a little louder.

Although there was no need for it, she had lowered her voice a touch.

It was because the information she had was so extraordinary that she felt she could speak about it only in hushed tones.

"A spy," the Earl said, his eyes widening.

"Yes," Odella affirmed. "It is a woman and she is extracting information from seamen that enables the French Navy to be – lying in wait for – their ships as they leave Port."

She spoke somewhat breathlessly and she realised that once again the Earl was finding it difficult to hear what she was saying.

To her surprise he then rose slowly to his feet.

"You say you have found a spy!" he said, determined to make sure of it himself. "Well, I have somebody with me who you must tell your story to, as I cannot quite understand what you are saying."

He moved slowly towards the door.

Odella rose from her seat and hurried to open it for him.

As he passed through it, he said,

"Come with me, my dear. The gentleman I want you to meet is in my study. He is, in fact, the Marquis of Midhurst."

Odella obeyed him.

They walked very slowly through the hall and down the corridor that led, as she knew, to the Earl's study.

It was with difficulty that she managed to walk as slowly as he did.

She felt that she wanted to run simply because precious time was passing and nothing yet was being done to save the men whom Madame Zosina was ready to send to their deaths.

It seemed a long time before they reached the study door and once again Odella opened it so that the Earl could go in first.

She was aware that a man was standing at the window.

As the Earl entered the room, it took him a few moments to realise where his guest was. He first looked towards the chairs in front of the fireplace where he had left him.

Then, as the Marquis of Midhurst turned around at the window, he said,

"My Rector's daughter has just called on me with a strange story that I think you ought to hear. I will therefore leave you together and I will tell my butler to bring you some wine."

He then moved back into the corridor as he spoke and Hodgson, who had followed them, closed the door.

Odella looked at the Marquis of Midhurst with interest.

She had, of course, heard of him and had read what the newspapers had reported about his two medals for gallantry in the war.

As she walked towards him, she thought that there was something overwhelming about him that she had not found in any other man.

She could not explain it to herself, but she felt as if his vibrations made him seem taller than he was. She thought that even in a crowded room one would have quickly been aware of him.

The Marquis, in point of fact, was rather annoyed at the way that the Earl had left him.

It was just when he was trying to explain to him why he had called so unexpectedly.

Aware of the Earl's deafness, he had been speaking louder than he usually did.

Then the butler had come to the Earl's side to say that a Miss Odella wished to see him urgently.

He had been surprised when the Earl, instead of saying she must wait, rose to his feet and went slowly from the room.

And now instead of listening to what he had come to relate to him, the Earl had left the Rector's daughter alone with him.

As Odella reached him, he saw that she was very young and surprisingly lovely, but she was wasting his time.

He was well aware from what the Prime Minister and Viscount Castlereagh had said that it was not talk that was needed at this moment but action.

The Marquis, therefore, said in a somewhat uncompromising voice,

"You must excuse me if I now go and join my host, because I have very little time at my disposal."

"I can understand that," Odella said, "but what I was trying to tell the Earl is that I have discovered – a spy in – Portsmouth."

For a moment the Marquis thought that she must be joking.

She had lowered her voice as she spoke and the Marquis said with a slight twist of his lips,

"How did you know he was a spy? Was he draped in black and prying in a manner which made you feel suspicious?"

Odella stared at him.

Then, as she realised that he was making fun of her, she turned and walked towards the door.

She had almost reached it when the Marquis said sharply,

"Where are you going?"

"To find somebody, my Lord," Odella replied, "who will listen to what I have to say and understand that I am trying to save the lives of the men who will be sailing from Portsmouth to join the Duke of Wellington's Army now in France."

As she finished speaking, she reached out towards the handle of the door.

She was on the point of opening it, when the Marquis called out,

"Stop!"

It was a command and almost despite herself she turned back towards him.

"Are you serious in what you have just told me?" he asked.

"I would not have come here immediately to bother the Earl if I did not think that what I have discovered is not merely serious but extremely urgent!" Odella retorted.

"Then I must apologise to you. Please come back and tell me about this."

Just for a moment Odella thought that she could not be placated so easily and then she remembered that precious time was passing.

Even now the ships leaving Portsmouth would be unaware that the enemy was waiting to attack them.

Slowly therefore she walked back into the room and towards the Marquis.

When she reached him, she looked at him with an unmistakably hostile expression in her eyes.

"Suppose we sit down?" the Marquis suggested in a quiet voice. "Please forget what I said and tell me in detail exactly why you are here."

Odella wanted to say that she preferred to stand and then, because he somehow seemed to force her to obey him, she sat in the nearest chair.

"I went to Portsmouth this morning," she began, "to do some shopping. When my maid and I were driving through the main street, we encountered a circus parade. They have set up their tents in Lincoln Field."

She found it hard to look at the Marquis as she spoke. Her mother had always told her that she should look at the person who she was talking to.

She was, nevertheless, aware that he was listening to everything she was saying.

She then went on with the story, telling him how, when she had done her shopping, she and her maid had gone to where the circus was performing.

She told him how they had decided first to consult Madame Zosina, the fortune-teller.

She described the arrangement of the chairs inside the tent, how the seamen were going in one by one to have their fortunes told and finally how she had been able to listen to what was being said when it was her turn next.

When she disclosed what she had overheard, the Marquis sat down in a chair beside her.

"You could hear them quite easily?" he asked.

It was the first time he had spoken since she had begun her story.

"Not easily," Odella replied, "because Madame Zosina spoke in a very soft voice. But I was aware, because I too can tell fortunes, how clever she was at extracting information from them without the seamen having the slightest idea what she was doing."

She paused to catch her breath before she went on,

"When the last seaman came out, a soldier asked if he could go in before me, as he had to be back in his Barracks by four o'clock."

She went on to explain what had been said to the soldier and how he had replied.

Ever since she had been small she had been taught by her father to memorise poems and quotations accurately and she had been made to learn the Collects for every Sunday from the time she could read.

Her father liked her to sing the well-known hymns in the Church without referring to her Hymn Book.

"The more you use your brain, the better it works," was one of the Rector's favourite sayings.

Odella thought as she repeated to the Marquis what she had overheard that it was exactly what had been said.

Only occasionally had there been a word that she had missed.

She finished by explaining how the soldier, in the same way as the sailor, had been given a so-called talisman, which would 'keep him safe'.

"What did you do then?" the Marquis asked.

"My maid, Emily, who had accompanied me, went in next," Odella related.

"And did Madame Zosina use the same technique on her?"

"No, my Lord, she did not. She used the usual patter of all fortune-tellers whether they are speaking the truth or not."

"Do you claim to be speaking as an authority since it is something you do yourself?" the Marquis wanted to know.

Odella gave a little laugh.

"I am hardly an authority, but I do tell fortunes at our village Bazaars and people believe what I tell them. And in ninety-nine cases out of one hundred my predictions come true."

"So you were aware that Madame Zosina was an expert at drawing out the secrets that simple men had sworn not to reveal to anyone."

"They had not the slightest idea that they were betraying their comrades or themselves," Odella said quickly. "They merely thought that she was using some magic that is outside the rules and regulations given to humans."

"I suppose you know," the Marquis said quietly, "that what you have told me is vitally important and something has to be done about it immediately."

"That is precisely why I am here," Odella replied. "My father is away from home and will not be back for about a week. So the only other person I could turn to was therefore the Lord Lieutenant."

The Marquis rose from his chair and walked across the room. And Odella realised that he was pondering what she had just told him.

She could not help thinking that he really was one of the most handsome men she had ever imagined.

She then wondered, although she knew that the Marquis's home was quite some distance away, whether her father and mother had known his parents.

He was obviously older than she was and so she thought that he must be twenty-eight or twenty-nine.

She would never have met him at children's parties, as she had met most of the other young men of any social standing in the County of Hampshire.

The Marquis turned around once again and walked towards her.

"I have been thinking over what you have told me," he said. "What we have to find out, and this is the key to the whole problem, is who Madame Zosina passes on the information to that she extracts from those who are sailing in the ships that leave the Port."

"I realise that," Odella said, "and it must be that person who by some means alerts the French Navy."

The Marquis nodded and she urged him,

"Please, my Lord, do something quickly! I cannot – bear to think of those men sailing to their – deaths before they have even had a chance of – firing a shot at the enemy."

"I am trying to plan what we can do," the Marquis answered, "and I am hoping, Miss Odella, I don't know your other name, that you are brave enough and patriotic enough to do what I suggest."

Odella looked at him in surprise.

"W-what are you – asking *me* to – do?" she enquired nervously.

"I am just working it out in my mind, but if I could arrange for Madame Zosina to be taken suddenly ill, would you take her place, tell the fortunes of those who consult her and eventually meet whoever it is she contacts to pass on her traitorous information?"

Odella's eyes opened wide.

"T-take – Madame Zosina's place?" she murmured.

"You say you can tell fortunes," the Marquis said, "and you described Madame Zosina as wearing a *yashmak* in the circus parade. It would be quite easy for you to take her place, as the public does not see her face properly."

Odella gave a little gasp, but she did not interrupt as the Marquis went on,

"I may be wrong, but I do speak from long experience when I say that it is doubtful if Madame Zosina actually knows the name of the Agent to whom she passes her information and she has probably never really seen him."

"H-how can that be – possible?" Odella asked.

"She is sure to be approached at night. I think it unlikely he would send a go-between, since he would trust nobody but himself with such vital information."

The Marquis made an expressive gesture with his hands.

"I am only guessing, of course, but we have to play the situation by ear and must always be ready to expect the unexpected."

"But – how – how can I do what you – want?" Odella asked him.

Even as she spoke she knew in her heart that it was not impossible.

Her father was away and, if the Marquis could arrange to collect her from the Rectory, Mrs. Barnet would not be particularly surprised if she told her that she was going to stay with a friend.

At the same time it was terrifying.

How could she play a part which might be a dangerous adventure or perhaps even be considered ridiculous by any of her father's friends if they discovered what she had done?

As if he knew exactly what she was thinking, the Marquis said quietly,

"You will be doing this for England. Would you ever sleep peacefully again if you knew that you had let these two ships, if not many more, go to the bottom of the sea without trying to prevent it?"

"S-surely, there must be – someone better – than me?" Odella objected.

"Who?" the Marquis asked sharply. "You have been clever enough to discover what has been puzzling both the Prime Minister and Viscount Castlereagh for a long time now."

His voice deepened as he continued,

"I am trusting you with my secret, Miss Odella, when I tell you that I have come here from London specially to find out how our ships are being shadowed as soon as they leave Port and are then attacked when they reach the open sea. By what seems a miracle you have already brought me the answer I need when I had expected that it might take me weeks or even months."

Odella's eyes were very wide in her small pointed face as she observed,

"It – does seem as if – God meant me to learn what Madame Zosina was – doing."

"I believed all the time that we were fighting our way through both Portugal and Spain that God was on our side," the Marquis informed her quietly. "On many occasions when we found ourselves in an ambush that threatened to annihilate us all, we escaped only by what seemed to be Divine protection."

Odella gave a deep sigh.

"Then I will – try to do what you – suggest, but please – please explain to me very – carefully exactly what will happen – because I am – very frightened."

"Of course you are," the Marquis said in a comforting manner, "but I will make it as easy as I can and I promise you one thing and it is that you will not be unguarded. There will be men within call ready and waiting in case anything should go wrong."

He spoke in a way that made it seem to Odella that he had already taken command and the whole plan was falling neatly into place in his mind.

"What I am going to suggest to you now," he said, "is that you go home and say nothing to anyone, not one single word, of what is to happen."

Odella was listening to him intently.

She clenched her fingers together because she felt as if every nerve in her body was alert and she knew that she must keep her self-control and not interfere or argue.

"Tomorrow morning," the Marquis was saying, "you will receive a letter asking you to stay the night, or perhaps two nights, with a friend whose name you will give me. Whoever is in your household will want to know where you are going. Is your mother there?"

"N-no, my mother is – d-dead," Odella replied, "and, as I told you, my father is – away. There are only the servants. They have looked after me for many years and are naturally – interested in everything I do."

"Very well," the Marquis said. 'They, of course, must not be in the least suspicious that you are doing anything unusual. Give me the name of someone who lives on the far side of Portsmouth from your home, which is the direction that they will see you travel."

Odella realised that he was thinking of every detail and she proposed,

"Mrs. Grayson is an old friend of the family and I did stay with her last year for a garden party she was giving."

The Marquis walked to the desk and, taking a piece of writing paper in his hand, wrote down the name.

"You will inform your household that Mrs. Grayson has asked you to stay and is sending a carriage for you at five o'clock. It will take you to the field where the circus is taking place and then you will go to Madame Zosina's tent, as you did today, and wait for your turn."

"I understand," Odella murmured more to herself than to the Marquis.

"There you will find a man whom you will allow to go in first," the Marquis continued, "preferably when there is no one else in the tent. Yet if there are others waiting, it cannot be helped. Do you understand?"

"Y-yes – "

"If you listen, as you did before, you will hear the man having his fortune told. Then he will invite Madame Zosina to drink to the success of what she has predicted for him."

The Marquis paused before he continued,

"When she drinks what he has offered her, he will leave her and you will take his place. A few seconds later she will collapse. Then you will call for a member of the circus to be fetched."

Odella thought just how embarrassing this would be.

At the same time she said nothing.

"When the owner or someone in authority does arrive, you will tell him that you were with Madame Zosina when it happened. You will say that you have had nursing experience and you realise that she has suffered a slight heart attack. You will suggest that she is carried to her caravan and you will go with her."

Odella was listening, her face now very pale.

"Then you will say," the Marquis went on, "that she may well be unconscious for several hours and you then offer to take her place. You will explain that you have had considerable experience as an amateur fortune-teller. If the circus people seem reluctant, you will say how much those who are waiting in the tent are looking forward to consulting Madame Zosina and how disappointed they will be if she is not available."

"That is true," Odella agreed.

"You can point out that if you wear her costume and *yashmak*," the Marquis said, "no one will doubt for a moment that it is not Madame herself who telling them their fortunes."

He paused.

"It – it does sound feasible," Odella admitted, "but – suppose that I am – denounced as an imposter?"

"Why should you be?" the Marquis asked sharply. "After all, when people go to have their fortunes told, they are thinking of themselves not of the figure gazing into her crystal ball."

Odella recognised that this was undoubtedly true.

"A-and – after that?" she asked the Marquis hesitantly,

"You wait until the session is finished, then go to Madame Zosina's caravan, where she will still be lying unconscious. You may have to spend the night with her and I can only hope that it will not be too uncomfortable."

He smiled at Odella before he went on,

"Equally I am very sure that she will be contacted by the Agent to whom she is passing on the secrets she has extracted from the seamen and the soldiers during the afternoon and supposedly that evening."

"Supposing – he does not – come?" Odella questioned.

The Marquis did not reply and after a moment she asked,

"Are you – s-saying I must stay on – still taking – Madame Zosina's place?"

"You will next be given by the man who had drugged her in the first place a small bottle containing another dose of what he gave her to drink. If you have not learnt what we want to know by then and she looks like coming round from her unconsciousness, you will have to give it to her."

Odella clenched her fingers until the blood seemed to leave them.

She wanted to scream at the Marquis that she would not do it – it was too much to ask – and far too frightening.

Yet she knew that, if she did so, he would despise her utterly.

Then she would for ever reproach herself as a traitor to her own country.

'There is nothing else I – can do,' she thought helplessly.

Next, in a different tone, the Marquis said quietly,

"I know it is a great deal to ask of you. But, if you had seen as many men die as I have, laughing and joking up until the last moment and suffering incredible hardships of which you, sleeping comfortably in your bed, have no knowledge, you would know, like me, that you would do anything *anything* to save the life of one single man."

"I have – said I will – do it," Odella murmured, "and I shall – pray that I will not – fail you."

"I think you are very brave," the Marquis said, "and I feel sure that if anyone can pull this off, and I admit that it is very difficult, then it will be you!"

Odella gave a little sigh.

"I-I will go home and I will – wait for the – the letter you are – sending me from – Mrs. Grayson."

The Marquis put out his hand, and said gently,

"You are the bravest woman I have ever met and, if we pull this off, I will see to it that a large statue is erected to you in Portsmouth Harbour."

Odella laughed, as he had meant her to do, and it broke the tension between them.

Then she asked,

"What am I to – say to – the Earl?"

"Leave his Lordship to me," the Marquis replied. "I shall tell him that you gave me some information which may or may not be helpful, but which I will certainly bear in mind."

He smiled at her before he added,

"Incidentally I no longer need his help now that I have yours."

"Now you are – worrying me – again," Odella said, "and please – please make sure that – nothing goes wrong."

"You have to trust me," the Marquis answered, "as my men trusted me. And without boasting I can truthfully say that I never failed them."

Odella walked towards the door and he opened it for her.

As they neared the hall, he said in a normal tone of voice for Hodgson's benefit,

"I know I have kept you talking for longer than I should have done, Miss Odella, and you want to get home. I will make your apologies to his Lordship and I hope we can meet again some day. When the peace bells are ringing, I will give a large party at Midhurst Manor."

"I shall look forward to it," Odella answered.

She said 'goodbye' to Hodgson and the Marquis escorted her to her carriage.

As Thompson drove off, she raised her hand in farewell.

No one watching, she thought, would suspect for a moment that they had been hatching a plot which could only have come out of a novel or perhaps even a melodrama performed on the stage.

'It cannot – be true! It just – cannot be true!' Odella whispered to herself as she drove away.

CHAPTER FOUR

When Odella was small, like most only children, she had an imaginary companion who was always with her.

Hers was a small boy called 'Mickie' and, as she grew older, Mickie grew with her.

He was still so much a part of her life that he gradually became in a way her Guardian Angel especially after her mother had died.

She asked his advice on a regular basis and begged his help whenever she needed it.

Now, as she went to bed, she was talking to Mickie as she had when she was very small.

He became familiar to everyone in the household and it was Mickie who was naughty and Odella who was good.

When she was six years old, she tried to jump the stream when it was swollen after a huge thunderstorm, fell in and was soaked from head to foot.

Her father was very angry with her and castigated her in no uncertain terms,

"It was extremely naughty of you to do anything so foolish."

"Mickie dared me to do it," Odella admitted.

"If Mickie suggests anything so dangerous in the future, he will have to be punished," the Rector said severely.

Odella put her head on one side and asked,

"How will you punish Mickie, Papa?"

"I will forbid him to play with you for a week," the Rector answered, "and, if he does not obey me, he will have to go away for ever."

"But I cannot lose Mickie – I cannot!" Odella had wailed.

"Then tell him to be good," the Rector admonished her.

That night when he was alone with his wife he said,

"I am beginning to believe in Mickie myself. To Odella he is so real that she convinces me that he actually is hovering in the background."

Mrs. Wayne laughed.

"I feel like that too. It is Mickie who does all the prankish things around here, but I do think that he has a great sense of humour."

Now, as she undressed and was getting ready for bed, Odella was talking to Mickie.

"Suppose I fail?" she said. "Yes, I know you will – help me, but it is – very dangerous, and yet it is something I *have* to do."

She gave a little sob before she went on,

"How can I let those men be – drowned or shot by – the French just because a wicked fortune-teller has – extracted secret information from them?"

As she pulled the sheets up to her chin, she said,

"Why did I – go there? If we had gone to the Big Top first, this would – never have – happened."

Almost as if Mickie was answering her, she knew that she had been specially chosen to help and to save her countrymen.

The French were hard, cruel and wicked and they had overrun and forced into subjection countries that were not theirs.

Napoleon had, however, abandoned his plan of invading England with men in barges. And Odella had thought as a child ten years ago that God had deliberately made the English Channel too rough for them to embark.

It must have been God who had chosen her, because she could tell fortunes, to prevent the spy from doing any further damage.

The spy and Madame Zosina enabled the French to sink ship after ship before it could accomplish its mission.

"You must – help me – Mickie, you must," Odella cried out as she tossed and turned.

In point of fact she slept very little, but kept waking up with a start, feeling that she should already have left for Portsmouth.

*

When morning came, there was a letter, which was found pushed under the front door.

Odella read it and told Mrs. Barnet that she had been asked by Mrs. Grayson to stay with her for one night perhaps two.

"That'll make a nice change for you. Miss Odella," Mrs. Barnet said. 'It's good for you to get out. You be lonely when the Master's away. Now what are you goin' to wear?"

This was something practical that had not occurred to Odella.

She allowed Mrs. Barnet to pack one of her prettiest evening gowns, which her mother had bought for her just before she had died. It was one that she had never had the chance of wearing as yet.

Mrs. Barnet chattered on, saying that it was time she went to some parties and danced as she used to when she was a child.

"All the boys I danced with in those days," Odella replied, "are now grown up and are either in the Army or the Navy."

As she said the last word, she gave a little shiver.

Suppose she made a mess of what she had to do? Suppose one of the men who would lose their lives was a boy she had played *Oranges and Lemons* with as a child?

She remembered how she used to enjoy *Musical Chairs* at all the local children's parties when the boys thought it fun to push the girls onto the floor and stop them sitting down on a chair.

She was not interested in what Mrs. Barnet was packing for her, but she had, however, given thought to the gown that she would wear to travel to Portsmouth.

The Marquis had told her to say that she had had nursing experience and she thought that most of her gowns made her look too young and rather frivolous.

She therefore chose a black gown that she had worn last when her mother had died. It had a coat to wear over it.

"What d'you want to wear that for?" Mrs. Barnet asked in astonishment. "Surely Mrs. Grayson'll think it a bit strange?"

"Papa does not believe in people mourning for a long period of time," Odella replied. "And Mama used to say our loved ones who had died were in Heaven and looking down on us and helping us."

She had gone on quickly,

"Mrs. Grayson might be shocked if I was not still in deep mourning and there is no point in upsetting her."

"No, I suppose not," Mrs. Barnet said. "But I likes you in your muslins, ever so pretty you looks in them."

"Thank you." Odella smiled.

In the afternoon she put on the bonnet that went with the black gown, which was nicely trimmed with black ribbons. It haloed her hair, which was the colour of sunshine and made her skin seem dazzlingly white.

When Odella looked at herself in the mirror, she had the idea that she did not look in the least like a working nurse. But she told herself consolingly that she did seem to have a little more authority.

At the last moment she remembered her father's spectacles that he wore in the summer when it was very hot.

Because he worked so hard at his research for the historical book he was writing, his eyes ached in the sunshine and he therefore had a pair of plain spectacles tinted that seemed to take away the glare.

Odella put them on her nose in the study and looked at herself in a gold-framed mirror, which had been a Wedding present when the Rector and his wife were married.

Now, she told herself, she certainly looked very much older and if she said that she was experienced in nursing, nobody was likely to contradict her.

Then, as she heard footsteps approaching, she hastily put the spectacles in her handbag.

Mrs. Barnet opened the door.

"The carriage be at the door. Miss Odella," she said, "your trunk's been put inside and I've added a hat box containin' a pretty bonnet in case you changes your mind and wants to look more like yourself."

Odella gave a little laugh.

"I promise you I will take off my black if and when I find it unnecessary."

She kissed Mrs. Barnet 'goodbye' and then waved to Emily, who was watching through the kitchen window.

Then she stepped into the plain, rather ordinary-looking carriage that was waiting for her outside the front door. She thought, however, that the coachman looked more mature than the average coachman.

He did not speak to her, but merely touched his hat.

They drove off, Mrs. Barnet waving as they went down the drive.

Odella knew that she was setting out on an adventure.

It was very intimidating because it was impossible to guess what would be the outcome.

Only after she had given a last long wave to Mrs. Barnet did she realise that there was an envelope on the small seat opposite her.

She picked it up and opened it.

Inside was a piece of paper on which was written,

"*HMS Heroic sails on Friday.*

HMS Victorious on Saturday."

She knew that these were the names of the two ships that she had to pass on to the spy.

She suspected that they were non-existent and that in fact no ships would be sailing on those particular days.

The envelope felt heavy and she then found that there was something in the bottom of it.

It was a very small bottle containing some ruby-coloured liquid.

She realised at once that this was a further dose of what the Marquis's man would give to Madame Zosina to make her unconscious.

She would have to repeat the dose if Madame Zosina came round before the Agent called to collect the information.

With a shudder of apprehension, Odella quickly put the envelope in her handbag.

Because she felt weak, she lay back against the padded seat.

She prayed fervently first to God and then to Mickie for all the help they could give her.

As the horse pulling the carriage gathered speed, she thought that she was travelling too fast to think clearly and yet she knew that she had to have all her wits about her and be very very careful not to make any silly mistakes that would ruin the mission.

The Marquis had promised her that she would be guarded, but it was difficult to guard somebody from a distance.

She was certain that if the Agent found out that he was being deceived, she would be what was called 'eliminated' in one way or another.

There had been so much talk of spies during the war that they had in some ways almost become a joke.

It was suspected that spies were brought to England by the smugglers and sometimes, it was believed, they rowed themselves across the English Channel.

Then they would hide in creeks and at river mouths, where they would be picked up by their associates.

As there had never been a spy in Nettleway, it was all just talk with no one having been in personal contact with one. However her father's research had taught him that this sort of thing had happened in the past.

Odella longed to discuss it with him now and anyway she desperately wanted and needed his advice.

At the same time she knew that, if he was aware of what she was doing, he would then undoubtedly have forbidden it.

She had always been very carefully protected and looked after as a child and since she had grown older, she had not been allowed to go anywhere without somebody being with her to chaperone her.

She realised that Mrs. Barnet had been surprised that Mrs. Grayson had not sent a maid to accompany her.

In fact after she had told Odella that the carriage had arrived, she had said as they walked down the passage to the hall,

"There's only the coachman, but I suspects that you'll be all right with 'im. He looks a sensible sort of man."

"Of course I will be all right," Odella had replied. "After all Mrs. Grayson does not live far away."

Mrs. Barnet made no reply, but she had given a sniff that told Odella without words that she thought Mrs. Grayson was not behaving quite as she should.

As they neared Portsmouth, Odella wondered if the coachman knew exactly what was happening.

She very much wanted to ask him if he had received any special instructions for her from the Marquis.

They were soon moving through traffic and there were quite a number of people on the pavements as they drove towards Lincoln Field, which was not far from the Harbour.

It was a large piece of wasteland which had never been cultivated and was used on all sorts of different occasions by the townsfolk of Portsmouth

The Flower Show took place there and there were Army Parades that were too large for the Barrack square.

Occasionally there was a mill that attracted too large an audience to be accommodated anywhere else in the town.

The last one, Odella remembered, was when Tom Scott, who was the champion fighter of England, had fought the champion of Portsmouth and not unexpectedly had been the easy winner to rapturous applause.

They arrived at Lincoln Field.

It was then that Odella realised that the Marquis had arranged for her arrival to coincide with the start of the performance in the Big Top.

She could hear the music of the band and the loud noise of excited voices.

There were a good number of small boys hanging about outside. They were trying to get a glimpse of the animals as they were led into the arena.

Some of the bolder boys were lying flat on the ground in an attempt to peep under the wall of the tent. And there were several attendants attempting to shoo them away.

The rest of the field was quiet except for the chatter of some children who were sitting on the steps of the caravans, which were parked some distance away from the Big Top against a hedge.

The horses, the majority of them piebald, had been taken from their shafts. They were cropping the grass, some tethered by their legs while others just wandered about free.

The carriage did not stop but drove on and Odella realised that it was taking her to the other end of the ground.

Here were a number of tall trees, but it was too far from the Big Top for there to be any caravans parked there belonging to the circus itself.

The carriage drew up in the shade of a tree whose branches partially concealed it.

Odella did not move until the carriage door opened.

Then the coachman said, speaking in a quiet educated voice,

"I'll be staying here, miss, all night."

Odella understood and replied in a small voice,

"Thank – you."

"If you go now into the fortune-teller's tent," the man went on, "you will find a Naval Officer inside."

He then turned his attention to his horse, as if he obviously had no wish for Odella to ask him any questions.

She then stepped out of the carriage and a little way to her left there was a path that led from the road above the field and she realised that, if anyone should see her, it would look as if she had just come from the town.

She therefore walked across the field as quickly as possible and then took her time going towards the fortune-teller's tent.

As she had noticed yesterday, it was quite some way from the Big Top.

She then saw that there was an attractive and colourful caravan parked by itself a little higher up the field.

She guessed that this one belonged to Madame Zosina and it was where she would be carried when she was unconscious.

It was still early in the evening and Odella expected that there would not yet be many people in the fortune-teller's tent.

A man stood at the entrance from whom she had to purchase a ticket.

He was obviously a Romany with long dark hair and dark eyes, but he was getting on in years and, despite his colourful shirt, he did not look at all interesting.

He took the money that Odella had offered him for her ticket without saying anything.

He handed her the ticket and politely drew aside the entrance flap of the tent for her to go inside.

There were only two people sitting there waiting.

The one nearest the glittering curtain that hid Madame Zosina was a young girl.

Next to her was, Odella knew, the man she was looking for.

He was dressed in naval uniform, that of an Officer rather than an ordinary seaman.

He was older than the young men who had been waiting ahead of Odella the previous day.

She sat down in the chair next to him and, as she expected, he totally ignored her.

He merely kept his eyes on the curtain behind which was the fortune-teller.

Three or four minutes passed before the curtain opened and a young man came out. He was a village type, simple and obviously excited by what he had just been told.

He put out his hand to the young girl sitting there.

"'Tis all right, Kitty," he said, "we'll get our own way."

"You're sure of that?" she asked.

"'Er says so and 'er knows," he replied. "Come on, there be no point in wastin' any more time around 'ere."

"I've not 'ad me fortune told," Kitty objected.

"You're fortune be my fortune!" the young man insisted. "Now, come on, I ain't 'angin' around 'ere no more."

He next pulled her somewhat roughly from the tent.

The Naval Officer then stood up and went behind the glittering curtain.

Odella moved up to the seat that Kitty had vacated so that she could hear what was being said inside.

In the same way that Madame Zosina had extracted information from the seamen and the soldier yesterday, she spoke in her seductive voice as she then went into action with her usual routine.

"You have a great career ahead of you," she began. "One day you will be famous and remember it was me who told you so."

"That's why I've come to see you," the Officer said.

After a few more questions he told her that there was just a chance, only a chance, that he would be promoted.

"You will be promoted not once but many times before you are finished with the Navy," Madame Zosina predicted. "Now, let me see you are going to get the chance to show how brave you are in an emergency."

Then she began to draw him out as to what he would be doing and where he was going.

It was all done very cleverly again.

Odella felt that anyone listening closely to Madame Zosina would be hypnotised into telling her anything she wished to know.

The Naval Officer allowed her to play her game to the full.

When she 'guessed' the name of the ship that he would be sailing in, he then asked in astonishment,

"How could you know that?"

"It's all here in my crystal ball," she replied. "And now to make you safe as you cross the English Channel, I will send with you my magic powers."

She promised to be thinking of him and using her magic from the time he set sail from Portsmouth until he arrived at his destination.

'There will be a skirmish or perhaps a battle when you land," Madame Zosina said, "but under your leadership your men will triumph and you will be rewarded."

Odella heard the Naval Officer give a sound of excited satisfaction and thought how well he was acting.

"You have told me just what I wanted to know," he said as Madame Zosina sat back, apparently exhausted. "Now I've brought with me a bottle of the best claret that my father, who's a wine merchant, gave me. It's a claret that's been drunk by His Royal Highness the Prince Regent himself and I want you to drink my health and to the future you have foretold for me."

"I will certainly do that," Madame Zosina agreed.

There was the sound of a cork being pulled from a bottle and then of wine being poured into a glass.

"Now, that is really something worth drinking," the Naval Officer said with satisfaction. "Please wish yourself the best while you drink it, as well as me."

Madame Zosina gave a little laugh.

"I will do as you say and you must do the same with me."

"I am ready to drink the bottle dry after what you have told me!" he enthused.

He must have held out the bottle for Odella heard a chink as if a glass touched it.

Then Madame Zosina toasted,

"To your health and happiness, sailor, and may you achieve all you wish for yourself."

"And everything you have wished me," the Naval Officer replied.

She must have drunk only half of what was in her glass because he said,

"Now, 'bottoms up' for good luck and if you leave that wine lying about, as sure as eggs is eggs, someone will sneak it away."

Madame Zosina laughed and then must have drunk all that was left in her glass.

The Naval Officer scraped back his chair and ventured,

"I'll be thinking about you all the way to France."

"As I will be thinking of you," Madame Zosina replied.

He came back through the curtain and to Odella's surprise did not even look at her.

He was carrying the bottle in his hand and sauntered along as if he was in no hurry to leave the tent.

As he passed the man who took the tickets, he said,

"That lady is a real marvel and that's the truth!"

The man did not reply and Odella, rising to her feet, went through the curtain.

As she might have expected, Madame Zosina was now sitting on what looked to her like a golden Throne.

On either side were two huge candlesticks. They were like those that Odella had seen in Roman Catholic Churches and the candles were all lit.

In front of Madame Zosina was a table and on it was a crystal ball, similar to the one she had carried in the circus parade. It was now set on an elaborate base to hold it in position.

Madame Zosina was still wearing her *yashmak*, but it was rather difficult to see anything clearly in the flickering candlelight.

Besides the crystal ball there was a pack of playing cards spread out on the table.

As Odella appeared, Madame Zosina asked her,

"Do you want me to tell your fortune by the cards or shall I look into my crystal ball and see what Fate has in store for you, my dear?"

"I would like the crystal ball, if you please," Odella replied.

She sat down on the seat in front of Madame Zosina.

"That is wise. The magic I see in my crystal ball comes directly – from the stars."

Madame spoke in a dreamy voice and then bent forward over her crystal ball.

She suddenly put her hand up to her forehead.

Then slowly, very slowly, she toppled forward, knocking the crystal ball from its base as she did so.

For a moment Odella did not move.

Then, when she realised that Madame Zosina was completely unconscious, she opened the curtain and ran to where the man was selling the tickets.

He had just handed one to a young woman and Odella said in a voice that she hoped no one else could hear,

"Madame Zosina has fainted! Get somebody to help me – carry her to her caravan."

The man looked at her in astonishment and then without saying anything more, Odella deliberately ran back into the tent.

She stopped to look back and saw that he was hurrying away.

With difficulty she raised Madame Zosina from where she had fallen forward onto the table.

Then tentatively, because she did not like touching her, Odella pulled the *yashmak* away from her face.

She was not expecting her to be young, but certainly not as ugly as she was.

Now she understood exactly why she wore a *yashmak*.

Her face was thin and lined and Odella guessed that, when she removed the glittering crown and veils, her hair would be grey.

She waited as patiently as she could.

It seemed to her a particularly long time before the man who took the tickets returned with a woman.

They entered through the back of the tent behind Madame Zosina.

"Now then, what's all this about?" the woman asked in a hostile voice.

"Madame Zosina was about to tell my fortune," Odella explained, "when she collapsed. I am in fact a qualified nurse and I have been thinking that perhaps she has suffered a slight heart attack."

"A heart attack?" the woman shrieked. "Now, why on earth should she have that, I'd like to know?"

"It can happen quite suddenly," Odella replied, "and, as a nurse, I can tell you that there is no need for it to be serious. In an hour or so she may well be a great deal better."

"An hour or so?" the woman repeated. "That's a lot of use! There's already half-a-dozen people waitin' to have their fortunes told."

"We ought to take her to her caravan and let her rest," Odella volunteered. "When we are there, I have a suggestion to make that may well help you."

"I doubt that," the woman said, "but it's no use her stayin' here. Luke, you'd better lift her up and get her away quickly or everybody'll be askin' us questions that we don't want to answer."

"We don't want any of that, Mrs. Covey," Luke replied.

He picked up Madame Zosina quite easily in his arms. She was not a big woman, Odella saw, and he carried her out of the back of the tent.

Mrs. Covey followed and looked back at the people waiting to buy tickets and she was obviously wondering if they had noticed what was happening.

It was only a short distance to the caravan and Mrs. Covey hurried ahead of them to open the door.

Luke carried Madame Zosina inside and laid her down on the bed.

It was a prettily furnished caravan with a beautifully embroidered Spanish shawl thrown over the bed.

"Go back to the tent, Luke," Mrs. Covey ordered him sharply. "Take the tickets and, if she's not better soon, you'll have to give them their money back."

"All right, Mrs. Covey," Luke agreed, "but I don't know what I'm goin' to say to them."

"Say nothin'," Mrs. Covey added in a sharp voice.

Odella was kneeling down beside the unconscious woman.

She took the crown from her head and released the veil that covered her hair. It was dyed red and it made her lined face look even more grotesque.

Luke had then hurried away and Mrs. Covey turned to ask Odella,

"How bad is she?"

"I think she will be all right in a few hours and definitely by tomorrow morning."

'Tomorrow!" Mrs. Covey repeated with a shriek. "And what am I to say to those as wants to consult her?"

"I was just going to suggest to you," Odella replied, "that perhaps I could be of help. I could take her place."

"You? What do you know about it?"

"I just happen to be a fortune-teller. Not a famous one, of course, like Madame Zosina, but I am well known in my village for making predictions that come true. I tell the future at Bazaars in the summer and balls in the winter."

Mrs. Covey gave a gasp.

She must have once been a pretty woman, perhaps an equestrian ballerina, but now she was getting on for fifty and there were deep lines under her eyes.

"Do you really think you could take Madame Zosina's place?" she asked. "She's a good fortune-teller and people come for miles around to consult her."

"You don't want them to be disappointed and, I promise you, I can tell fortunes. They will have not the slightest idea, if I wear Madame Zosina's clothes, that it is not she who is predicting their future."

"It certainly seems as if it's Fate you should be here," Mrs. Covey remarked, "and we're expectin' a real big crowd tonight. They'll make ever such a big fuss if they can't spend their money learnin' about the future."

"It would be a great pity to disappoint them," Odella replied, "and, as I have nothing else planned for this evening, I shall be glad to give you a hand."

"We'll pay you, of course," Mrs. Covey said, "and we'll be grateful for your help."

"People will soon begin to ask what has happened," Odella pointed out. "You will have to help me to dress."

She started to take off her bonnet as she spoke and she was relieved when Mrs. Covey quickly divested the unconscious woman of her costume.

It was very like a cloak and beneath it Madame wore only a bodice and a petticoat not unlike what Odella herself was wearing.

She had thought that she would keep on her black gown. However Mrs. Covey undid it at the back and obviously expected her to take it off.

It did not take long for her to put on the glittering gown that had looked so spectacular when Madame Zosina drove through the town.

Mrs. Covey covered Odella's hair with the shining veil and placed on top of it the crown with its crimson feathers and sparkling gems.

She then stood back and looked at Odella in some satisfaction.

"No one'll guess in a million years you're not Madame Zosina herself," she said.

"Where is the *yashmak*?" Odella asked.

It was lying on the floor and Mrs. Covey picked it up.

"So that's what you calls it," she smiled. "I only knows it as a 'nose-veil' meself."

She laughed and Odella laughed with her.

Then she said,

"In case Madame has not recovered by the time I have finished, I had better stay here with her tonight. It would be a mistake for anyone, even members of the circus, to know that she is being impersonated."

"That's really kind of you," Mrs. Covey said. "And you're right, of course. If they talk, what they says will fly on the wind."

She made a gesture with her hands and went on,

"We'll have half of Portsmouth knowin' that Madame's bin taken bad and that'll put the takings down, I can tell you!"

"Then let's keep quiet about it," Odella suggested, "and, if I go back to the tent now, even Luke will think that Madame Zosina has recovered."

"Oh, Luke's safe enough," Mrs. Covey answered. "'I'll see he doesn't open his mouth."

She looked around the caravan.

"'I'll bring you some blankets and a pillow. You'll be comfortable enough on the floor and, as I've said, it be real good of you and somethin' I won't forget in a hurry – "

"I had better go to the tent," Odella interrupted hastily. "I can see from here that there are more people going towards it and so the sooner I can get to work the better."

"You're a real sport," Mrs. Covey declared, "and Zosina'll be ever so grateful. I promise you that."

Odella smiled at her.

"It will be a new experience to be dressed up like this. When it comes down to it, people always seem to ask the same questions about themselves."

"I bet they do," Mrs. Covey grinned, "and you tell them what they wants to hear."

She helped Odella, who was somewhat hampered by her flowing robes, down the steps of the caravan to the ground.

Then they walked quickly to the back of the tent.

As she went inside, Odella could hear people talking instead of sitting silently waiting for their turn.

She guessed that this was unusual and Luke must have told them that there would be an interval before Madame Zosina could see the next client.

Odella had only just settled herself on the golden Throne when she heard him say,

"Madame Zosina's now ready to receive the gentleman in the front row. Will everyone else please remain quiet."

There was an instant silence.

For a moment she stared at the piece of paper, thinking it rather odd.

Then she understood.

The Marquis had certainly thought of everything and he had obviously realised, as she had not, that the Agent would recognise her voice as being different from Madame Zosina's.

Odella was certain that the lozenges would not take away a sore throat but give her one.

'He is very efficient,' she told herself.

Then she shivered because everything that was happening was likely to lead her deeper than ever into the mire of deception.

She looked around at the things in the caravan and found a clock.

It was not a very expensive one, but it probably was more or less accurate and she saw that it was after eleven o'clock.

She went over to the window and saw that now all the lights on the Big Top had been extinguished.

There were only a few lit windows in the distance belonging to the other caravans.

This meant that the Agent might come to her at any moment and Odella knew only too well that she must be ready for him.

She wished now that she had brought a cloak with her as she knew that it was going to be cold if she had to go outside for any reason.

All day there had been a little warmth of very early spring in the air, but the nights were still very chilly and it would have been sensible, she reflected, if she had been wrapped up in one of her winter coats.

As she thought of it, she looked at the far end of the caravan and in a dark corner, there was hanging what looked like a cloak.

She took it down and found that it was exactly that, a black cloak with a hood at the back of it.

She had a distinct feeling that it was what Madame Zosina would put on to meet the man who she relayed her information to.

Whether this was true or not, Odella decided that it would be a wise move for her to wear it. She could pull the hood over her forehead and hide part of her face as well as her golden hair.

The Marquis had said it was unlikely that she would be able to see the face of the Agent, but she could not be sure.

She could only pray that she would meet him in the darkness so that, while she could not see him, he could not see her.

She spread the blankets on the floor and then propped the pillow up against the wall and wearing the cloak with the hood over her head, she settled down to wait.

To make sure that her face was hidden, she fastened the *yashmak* round her neck so that she could pull it over her nose at a moment's notice.

Then she had another idea.

She took the names of the ships from her handbag, read them several times to make certain that she would not make a mistake and then blew out the candle-lantern.

She had to grope her way back to her blankets and the pillow.

Once she was seated, she was aware that there was just a faint glimmer of light from the stars shining through the windows.

There was not a sound from Madame Zosina, although Odella well knew that she was breathing and was not dead, as she appeared to be.

'Help me, Mickie, *help me*!' Odella prayed in her heart.

She was aware, although she tried to be calm, that the fear of what was going to happen was steadily creeping over her.

It was moving through her breast and slowly up to her lips and she felt that, if the Agent did come, she would be unable to speak to him.

'He must be here – soon,' she reckoned.

She picked up one of the lozenges and put it into her mouth.

It did not taste very nice, but, as the Marquis had sent them for her, she forced herself to suck it.

When she had nearly finished it, she tried tentatively to say aloud,

"Hello."

There was no doubt that her voice sounded hoarse and unnatural.

'I am here ready and waiting,' she told herself, 'and the only thing missing is – the spy!'

If it had not been so frightening, she thought that she might have laughed at the idea.

She was just a country girl who had never done anything adventurous in her whole life.

And now here she was on her own disguised as another woman in a Romany caravan and waiting to talk to a French spy.

He was planning to destroy the ships that left from Portsmouth carrying men who were to join Wellington's Army.

Could anything be more fantastic?

And yet it was actually happening to her.

'I must be calm, very calm and – composed,' Odella told herself. 'Help me – Mickie – *help* – *me*!'

It was then that there was a knock on the caravan door.

It was loud, but a single knock.

For a moment Odella felt paralysed as if she could not move her limbs.

Then she forced herself to put up her *yashmak* over her nose as she had planned to do.

Slowly she rose and groped her way towards the door. She opened it and thought for a moment that she must have been mistaken.

There was no one there.

Then she saw that the man who must have knocked was moving up the path that led to the road.

With difficulty, because there was no moon, she could make out the outline of a carriage.

Almost as if someone was directing her, she knew what she now had to do.

She walked down the steps of the caravan and onto the ground and then closing the door behind her, she moved towards the man.

He waited for her to appear and, when he saw her coming along towards him, he walked on ahead of her.

When she reached the road, she could see, as she had expected, that there was a carriage drawn by two horses waiting there.

The man who had walked ahead was standing at the door of the carriage.

As she reached him, he opened it.

There was only darkness inside the carriage and Odella realised that there were blinds or curtains pulled over the windows.

She was obviously expected to enter and as she did so she was aware of a strong smell of brandy mixed with another smell that she could not for the moment identify.

Then a voice said,

"Do sit down Madame, on the little seat."

It was just beside her and as she did so, the door was closed and now there was complete darkness.

Odella put out her hand to steady herself and found that on the seat beside her there was a large box.

As she touched it, there was a rustling movement inside it and she gave what was almost a little scream.

"It be all right," the man said. "It's only our little feathered friends, who have suffered somewhat from the roughness of our sea crossing."

It was with almost a superhuman effort that Odella did not scream again.

Now she knew and now she understood what had puzzled her and the Marquis.

Feathered friends! Why had they not thought of that?

Unexpectedly another voice spoke up.

"If they can surmount the waves," he said, "so can I."

Odella had assumed that there would be only one man to speak to her and it came as a shock to realise that there were two men sitting on the back seat and this was the reason why she had been told to sit on the smaller one.

"Was it very rough?" the first man, who she thought must be the Agent, asked.

"*C'était formidable!*"

The answer came in French and he then asked in the same language,

"*Elle ne comprend pas français?*"

"Not a word," the Agent said in the same language.

He bent towards Odella and now she could smell even more strongly the brandy that he had been drinking.

"What have you to tell me, Madame?" he asked. "I apologise for being late, but, as you have just heard, the sea was very rough."

Odella reduced her voice almost to a whisper and even to herself it sounded very hoarse.

"I have two ships for you," she answered, "*HMS Heroic*, which sails on Friday and *HMS Victorious*, which is leaving on Saturday."

"That is very good and, as you know, there will be two victories, splendid victories!"

"I will give you a third," the Frenchman said, speaking in his own language, "and one that is greater than any that you have achieved."

"I do hope you are right," the Agent replied, also speaking in French, "but remember that Jacques and Henri tried and failed."

"But I am different," the Frenchman replied. "I have the *entrée*."

He spoke in a boastful tone and listening, Odella guessed that he had been drinking more than the Agent had.

Now she knew that the other smell that was mixed with the brandy was the smell of salt water.

She thought that when he crossed the English Channel that his clothes must have become very wet.

I have here your reward," the Agent said in English to Odella, "and, of course, there will be more when you have more information for me tomorrow night."

He was obviously feeling in his pocket for what he required and he brought something out and put it on Odella's lap.

She held it and he said,

"Ten golden goblins for the first ship and now ten for the second."

He started to feel in another pocket, but the Frenchman ordered,

"*Dépêchez-vous*! It is time we were on our way."

"The Post chaise is waiting here for you," the Agent replied, "and you will be in London easily by tomorrow afternoon."

"I must be sure of that," the Frenchman replied. "It is foolish to waste time."

The Agent found the other money and then passed it to Odella.

As she took it, he bent forward to knock on the window and the man outside opened the door.

As he did so, the Frenchman quickly slipped out and disappeared unobtrusively into the darkness.

He made his way, Odella supposed, to where the Post chaise was waiting for him.

Then Odella managed with a little difficulty, because she was on the edge of the seat, to step down onto the ground.

She had no sooner done so than the man slammed the door to, climbed up onto the box and picked up his reins.

The horses had been standing quite still and now, as he brought the whip down heavily on their backs, they moved off at great speed.

The wheels threw up dust and gravel.

It all happened so quickly that Odella was left standing on the side of the road holding the money she had been given.

It was over! They had gone!

It was then she started to run towards the trees, where she believed the carriage would be waiting for her.

She was terrified by what she had heard and also afraid that she would never be able to tell the Marquis about it.

The thought made her run faster than she had ever run before despite the fact that she was encumbered by the long black cloak.

She pulled down the *yashmak* so that she could breathe more easily and pushed back the hood so that she could see better.

With a sense of relief she saw that the carriage was there.

The driver must have seen her coming, for he was waiting with the door open.

She was breathless as she reached him and he helped her inside.

As she half-collapsed into the seat, she realised that someone else was present and she gave a shriek of terror.

"It's all right," came a quiet voice. "It is only me."

It was the Marquis.

Because she was so relieved, Odella threw herself against him, saying incoherently,

"Oh – Mickie – Mickie – save me! They will – kill me if – they find out!"

The Marquis put his arms around her and he could feel her trembling uncontrollably.

He lifted her legs up onto the seat beside him, holding her in his arms as if she was a child.

Because it was all over and she was now safe, Odella burst into tears.

She cried tumultuously and helplessly.

The Marquis just held her close, feeling her body trembling against him.

"It's all over," he kept saying. "You are safe and no one shall hurt you."

It was impossible for Odella to speak.

Only as she felt the carriage moving and she knew that she was being carried away did she force herself to stop crying.

"I-I – am sorry – I am – s-sorry," she murmured, "b-but it has been – so frightening – and now I know – what has p-puzzled you – he is using *pigeons*."

"Carrier pigeons!" the Marquis exclaimed. "My God, why did I not think of that?"

"They were – there in the – c-carriage in a box – you must not let him – use them."

"You are not to worry about it," the Marquis said. "The carriage is being followed."

His arms tightened for a moment around Odella as he said,

"How can I have been so stupid not to think of that myself? But it never occurred to me that they could be brought here in a smugglers' boat."

It was then that Odella thought of something else to tell the Marquis and she exclaimed,

"There was also a Frenchman with him who got out of the carriage before I did and slipped away into the darkness."

"A Frenchman?" the Marquis exclaimed in astonishment.

"Yes and when – the Agent said that – the ships I had named for him would give him two victories – the Frenchman said that he would – give him an even – greater victory!"

The Marquis stiffened.

"A greater victory?" he repeated. "Did he say what it was?"

"N-no but, when the Agent said that – Jacques and Henri had – failed, he – replied that he would – succeed because he had – the *entrée*."

The Marquis was silent for a moment.

And then he asked Odella,

"Did he say anything else?"

"No – only that he was in a hurry – and the Agent assured him that – a Post chaise was – waiting for him and he would be in – London by tomorrow afternoon."

There was silence for a moment.

"He was speaking in French. Was there anything you noticed about him in particular?"

"I could not – see either him or – the Agent," Odella replied. "They sat in the – darkness of the carriage with the windows – covered."

"But you listened?"

"Yes – and the Frenchman was – drinking a lot of – brandy. There was also the – smell of sea water – which at first I did not – recognise. It had been rough in the English Channel and his – clothes must have – been very wet."

"And his voice?" the Marquis prompted. "What about his voice?"

"It was deep – except when he – boasted. Then it rose quite a bit – and yes – his accent was definitely Parisian."

"And you yourself speak Parisian French?"

"Yes, my mother was most – insistent that I should be taught the – very best Parisian French – although it seemed somewhat unpatriotic to me."

"Nevertheless," the Marquis responded, "it has been of inestimable value and a blessing that we must be sincerely grateful for."

Odella wiped her eyes with the back of her hand and the Marquis took a handkerchief from his inside pocket and handed it to her.

"I-I am sorry I – c-cried," she stammered, "but – "

As she spoke, she realised that she was still in the Marquis's arms.

Her head was resting on his left shoulder while her body lay across him and, because it was dark and because it was comfortable, she had no wish for the moment to move.

All she could think about was that she was safe.

The Marquis was there and so no one could hurt her.

She had managed to deduce from the way the Frenchman had spoken that he intended to kill somebody.

It had seemed as if the point of a dagger was piercing her heart until the carriage had driven away and she was still alive.

"I don't want to frighten you," the Marquis said, "but you do know what we have to do now."

Odella gave a little cry.

"Oh – no! I cannot – do any more – I am – frightened, so very frightened and – if they had – realised I could understand French – I know that they – would have killed me!"

"I promised that I would protect you," the Marquis said, "and that is what I will continue to do. But you do understand, Odella, that only you can save His Royal Highness."

There was a sudden silence.

Then Odella whispered in a voice that he could hardly hear,

"D-did you – say – His Royal – H-Highness?"

"That is whom I believe the Frenchman has come to kill," the Marquis said. "The two men who you have mentioned had tried previously to assassinate him, but were caught and executed."

"Y-you don't think – this Frenchman will – succeed?"

"Not if we denounce him first."

"H-how can – we do – that?"

It was obvious that she was very afraid again for the Marquis could feel her trembling.

He held her closer.

"Now, listen, Odella," he said quietly, "all you have to do is to come with me now to London and attend a party that the Prince Regent is giving tomorrow night at Carlton House."

He paused for a moment as if to reflect before he continued,

"It will not be as large as the parties he usually gives, but large enough for a Frenchman who has somehow managed to get himself invited to the party to kill the Prince Regent when he is comparatively unguarded."

"You – you can stop him – without me!" Odella cried.

"How can I do that when it is not I who has heard his voice?" the Marquis enquired.

"But – I cannot – I cannot do any m-more – I am frightened – very very f-frightened!"

The words seemed to pour out of her lips and she hid her face against the Marquis's shoulder.

"You have been so incredibly brave," he said softly. "So wonderful! I don't know of any other woman who would have behaved with such courage or such *patriotism*!"

Odella drew in her breath.

There was a note of sincerity in the Marquis's voice which could not be mistaken.

She squeezed her eyes to try to prevent herself from crying again.

Then she said in a whisper,

"I-I will do what – you want – but you will have to – help me."

"I *will* help you. I will be beside you and I promise you that no one shall harm you."

There was silence and Odella could feel that the horses were moving much more quickly.

Like a child who is frightened of everything, she asked pathetically,

"Wh-where are we – g-going?"

"We are going to my house because, if you remember, your servants would think it very strange that you did not stay the night with Mrs. Grayson as they had expected."

"And – when we get – there?" Odella enquired.

"We will leave for London at once. It will not be an easy journey, but I will make you as comfortable as possible. Then you must try to sleep."

Odella could think of nothing more to say.

She wanted to expostulate that she could not go to London alone with the Marquis and she then thought that it would sound particularly foolish when she had done so many things for him already.

It suddenly occurred to her at this moment how improper it was to be lying in the arms of a man she hardly knew.

And yet he seemed to fill her whole life.

She made a little movement.

As if he understood, he set her down beside him and then pulled a fur-lined rug over her knees.

Then he took her hand and held it in both of his.

"We have to be very clever, you and I," he said, "and you must remember every word the Frenchman spoke and every intonation in his voice so that you will recognise it instantly when you hear it again."

"I-I will try – I really will – try," Odella promised.

"There is something I do want to ask you," the Marquis said in a rather different tone of voice.

"What is – it?" Odella enquired nervously.

"When you climbed into the carriage just now, you called me 'Mickie'. What made you do that?"

"He was – in my mind – because I had been talking to him all day about what I – had to do."

"And – who is he?" the Marquis asked.

Now there was a harsh note in his voice.

She was aware that he suspected she had been discussing with somebody else what he had told her must be completely secret.

"He is – someone I – invented when I was a child," Odella explained, "but now I – think of – him as my – Guardian Angel."

"Your Guardian Angel!" the Marquis repeated slowly.

"That is strange, because 'Mickie' was what my mother always called me."

Odella's eyes opened wide.

"Your – mother called you – 'Mickie'?"

"My Christian name is Michael," the Marquis told her.

"Oh – !"

Odella could not think of anything else to say.

It seemed to her as if, in some extraordinary manner, Mickie, her playmate, her friend and finally her Guardian Angel had become one with the Marquis.

She could not put it into words.

Then, as she felt his fingers tighten on hers, she just knew that it was what had happened.

*

It did not take more than half an hour for them to reach Midhurst Manor.

By the time they arrived, Odella was sound asleep.

When the Marquis realised that she could no longer stay awake, he had moved her again.

She now lay flat out on the seat with a cushion at her head and covered by the sable rug.

The Marquis seated himself on the smaller seat and was aware that she was completely and utterly exhausted.

He guessed that she had not slept the night before and the drama of what had happened that evening had taken its toll on her.

The carriage drew up smartly beside a long flight of stone steps that led up to the front door.

The Marquis stepped out and he ordered one of the footmen to waken the housekeeper.

"Mrs. Briggs be already waitin' on the stairs, my Lord," the young man replied, "in case you required her."

The Marquis did not say anything.

He reached inside the carriage and gently lifted Odella up in his arms.

She was so light that he had no difficulty in carrying her up the steps, into the hall and up the carved staircase to the first landing.

Mrs. Briggs was already there.

When she saw that the Marquis was carrying a young woman in his arms, she asked no questions.

She merely went ahead to open the door of one of the guest rooms and the footman who had followed the Marquis carried a lamp.

The Marquis laid Odella down on the bed.

"Let the young lady rest undisturbed while I have something to eat," he ordered.

"Shall I undress her, my Lord?" Mrs. Briggs asked her.

The Marquis shook his head.

"We are leaving for London as soon as fresh horses can be brought to the door. Arrange for blankets and pillows to be put in the front of the travelling chariot."

"Very good, my Lord."

Mrs. Briggs hurried away.

The Marquis stood still for a moment, looking down at Odella.

It was quite impossible, he thought to himself, that any woman could look more lovely, childlike and untouched by the wickedness and cruelty of the world.

And yet she had behaved with a bravery that he had never found in any other woman.

Then, because he knew that he must not linger, he hurried from the room.

Going downstairs rapidly, he started to give his orders.

CHAPTER SIX

Odella thought that her bed was moving round the room and she wondered what was happening.

She opened her eyes and for a moment she thought that she must still be dreaming.

She was lying down and yet she could see the Marquis just where her feet ended.

It was then she realised that she was in a travelling chariot that was proceeding at a very fast pace.

She made a little sound and the Marquis turned his head to look at her.

"Where – am I?" Odella asked.

"We are now driving to London," he replied. "You have been snoring all the way and I thought you would never wake up!"

"I don't snore!" Odella retorted indignantly and then realised that he was teasing her.

"You were like a quiet little mouse," he conceded, "and there is no reason for you to wake up. Just relax and go to sleep again and I will take you to London safely."

It seemed incredible to Odella that she had not realised that he must have carried her from the carriage that they had left Portsmouth in and into the travelling chariot.

She could remember that she had cried and that he had comforted her thoughtfully.

Now, unbelievably, they were on their way to London to try to save the life of the Prince Regent.

As if he knew that she was going over in her mind what had happened, the Marquis said,

"You are not to worry yourself. I have everything planned and, if nothing else, you will enjoy seeing Carlton House."

"You mean – I will have to – go there?" Odella questioned.

"We are going to a party that His Royal Highness is giving," the Marquis replied. "I had thought that I would be so busy in Portsmouth that I would have to miss it. Now I can take you and you will find it really spectacular."

"But – how can I – ?" Odella began, thinking as any woman would that she had nothing to wear.

Then she remembered that Mrs. Barnet had put an evening gown in her trunk that she was supposedly taking to Mrs. Grayson's house.

At the same time it was fascinating to think that she was to see Carlton House, which she had heard so much about and read of in the newspapers and magazines.

She lay back against the pillows that she knew the Marquis must have propped up behind her.

As she did so, she was aware that she was not wearing the black cloak that belonged to Madame Zosina. She was wearing a different one that was lined with fur and trimmed with ermine.

It certainly kept her warm, as did the fur rug that covered her legs.

Because she was small, there was just room, even though the Marquis was driving, for her to recline on the seat of the travelling chariot.

A groom was accommodated behind somewhat precariously and she knew this because she had seen one of these chariots when her uncle had travelled in one to visit her father.

If the groom was lucky, he also had a hood to pull over his head when it rained.

But she could not see him and it was a strange feeling to be alone with the Marquis and travelling faster than she had ever been driven before.

She was aware that the chariot was drawn by four horses and the Marquis was driving with an expertise that she knew would have impressed her father.

He was wearing an overcoat with a high collar.

She could see his features silhouetted against the sky and she thought again that he was the most handsome man she had ever imagined.

He was just as she thought Mickie would look if she could actually see him.

"We are lucky," the Marquis remarked, "that the moon has come out and we can travel as fast as we could if it was daylight."

"Will it take us a long time to reach London?" Odella asked him.

She was remembering that the Agent had claimed that the Frenchman would get there in the afternoon.

"Not at the pace we are travelling," the Marquis replied. "Very shortly we will change horses and you will have something to eat. I feel sure you are hungry after all you have been through."

Odella recalled that she had not eaten the sandwiches or drunk the milk that had been left for Madame Zosina and she had been too frightened to eat anything while she was waiting for the Agent to arrive.

Now she was feeling empty.

It would be very nice to have just a little to eat, although she wondered what would be available in the middle of the night.

Now that the moon was out, everything was very beautiful and the road ahead looked like a silver streak winding away in the distance in front of them.

The Marquis's team was extremely well trained and because he drove them so brilliantly, they moved in a manner that prevented the chariot from bumping or swaying unnecessarily.

Lying back against the pillows, Odella thought that this was all part of an adventure that she would always remember.

Perhaps one day she would write the whole story down in a book.

She tried hard not to think of what awaited them at the end of the journey.

She was afraid, really afraid, that she would not recognise the Frenchman's voice.

And if he managed to kill the Prince Regent, it would be all her fault.

"Stop worrying!" the Marquis urged her quietly. "Enjoy this beautiful night and know that there are no carrier pigeons leaving Portsmouth today, or on any other day!"

"You are – sure that your – men will have – caught the Agent by now?" Odella asked tremulously.

"I was assured that they are the best men available," the Marquis replied, "and I cannot believe that your brilliance in discovering what was happening will go unrewarded."

Odella was silent for a moment.

Then she asked,

"And what – will happen to – Madame Zosina?"

"She will already have been collected from the caravan where we left her and taken to prison."

Odella gave a little cry.

"She will – not be – executed?"

"You are not to worry about it," the Marquis said firmly. "Forget the fortune-teller and concentrate only on what lies ahead for us, which is, of course, that you must look beautiful and shine at Carlton House."

To his surprise Odella laughed.

"Are you really expecting a raw girl from the country, who has never been to a party in London, to shine among all the sparkling glamorous women who, I have been told, surround the Prince Regent?"

She sounded completely unaffected and unselfconscious and the Marquis thought that she was very different in this way as she was in so many others.

What was more, she obviously had a keen sense of humour.

"I promise that you will shine," he said. "And if you feel the gown you have with you is not smart enough for the occasion, we will beg, borrow or steal one that is!"

Again Odella laughed.

"I am not surprised that you win all your battles," she said. "Confidence, my father says, is something one always needs to be successful in life."

The Marquis agreed with her.

At the same time he was aware that perhaps he was being over-optimistic.

Could it really be possible for this young girl to recognise the voice of a man she had heard only once before and in the dark?

And what was more, he is a foreigner?

As she had been so frightened, it would have been difficult for her to think of anything but the danger that she was in personally.

He thought as he drove on in the night that Fate had certainly played into his hands.

He had gone to Portsmouth thinking that the Prime Minister and Viscount Castlereagh had set him an impossible task. And there was only the faintest hope of his being successful in this mission.

They had all their people trying to discover why the ships that had left after dark should, the moment they were in the open sea, be attacked by the French Navy.

It had never struck any of them that the information was being conveyed to the French by carrier pigeons.

Then, before he had even begun his investigation or explained to the Earl of Portsmouth exactly what he required, Odella had arrived and she had given him the amazing information that she had discovered a spy.

'She is certainly a gift from the Gods,' the Marquis mused to himself.

Because he was feeling so grateful to her, he was really determined that she would enjoy herself at Carlton House.

He was quite certain that her beauty, which had astounded him, would not go unnoticed by the sophisticated clique surrounding the Prince Regent.

Then he told himself that it would be a great mistake for her to be spoiled or to become self-conscious.

He glanced down at her and he could see her very clearly in the bright moonlight that was shining into the carriage.

She was looking at him with wide eyes that seemed to reflect the stars.

'She is lovely, absolutely lovely!' he told himself.

Yet he thought that it would be a major error if, like so many other women, she fell in love with him.

As the daughter of an obscure country Parson, she could hardly play any part in his life in the future.

But he had no wish to leave her, perhaps broken-hearted, when she was no longer of any use to him.

He was not being conceited, he was being honest with himself.

He knew how many women, like Lady Georgina, had fallen wildly in love with him as soon as he so much as looked in their direction.

But Lady Georgina, whom he had made his mistress, was one thing.

A pure untouched young girl from a Rectory was something very different.

The Marquis knew that he must marry one day and have an heir. But there was no hurry and, after the strenuous years of war, he wanted to be free to enjoy himself as a bachelor.

He had found so far that the women he met in London were like beautiful flowers. They were only too eager for him to pluck them while they bloomed.

But they accepted it more or less resignedly when they faded and he then turned to find a different flower in another direction.

The Marquis had managed so far in his life never to prolong a love affair once it began to bore him.

The majority of women, like Lady Georgina, knew that, if they lost him, there would be nothing that they could do about it but accept it as inevitable.

Of course there were indeed times, the Marquis would fully admit, when there had been tears, rage and recriminations.

He had not listened to them and he was sure, cynically, that there was always another man ready to take his place as soon as he left.

Yet now he was worried about Odella.

He knew perceptively that, if she did fall in love with him, it would be a very different emotion from that which he aroused in women like Lady Georgina.

To Odella love would be something sacred.

What else would she expect from a man whom she confused in her mind, or was it in her heart, with her Guardian Angel?

'I must be very very careful not to hurt her,' the Marquis told himself. 'When she goes back to the Rectory, she must just have happy memories of this adventure and of her time in London with which to beguile the man she will ultimately marry.'

*

The Marquis drove his horses into the yard of a coaching inn.

Odella, who had not spoken for quite some time, asked him,

"Are – we stopping – here?"

"I promised you something to eat," the Marquis replied.

"But surely – everyone will be – asleep at this late hour?"

He smiled as he drew his horses to a standstill and then two ostlers came running from an adjacent stable.

"I have sent one of my grooms to ride cross-country," the Marquis explained, "which is quicker than going by road as we did, to warn them of our arrival. I shall be very annoyed if my orders are not carried out!"

"You think of everything, my Lord!" Odella exclaimed.

"For the moment I am thinking of you. So hurry inside and I expect you will find a maid waiting for you."

A maid was indeed waiting for Odella.

She took Odella up the wooden staircase to a bedroom where the candles were already lit and there was hot water to wash in.

Now Odella could see the cloak that she had been lent by the Marquis was even grander than she had thought it to be.

It was of Royal-blue velvet, trimmed with ermine and lined with the softest and warmest fur.

As she took it off, she wished that she had something more glamorous with her than her plain black gown to wear.

But she did not bother about herself for too long, knowing that the Marquis would be in a hurry to continue their journey to London.

When she went down the stairs, she was taken into a private room. A large log fire was burning in the chimney and a table was laid in front of it.

The Marquis was looking exceedingly smart in his tight champagne-coloured pantaloons and his Hessian boots were so highly polished that Odella was sure that one could see one's face in them.

He smiled at her as she came into the room and, pulling up a chair, suggested,

"Sit down, Odella. I have ordered what I believe you will enjoy and then we must be on our way."

The hot soup was delicious as was the well-cooked trout that followed it.

There was champagne to drink, which Odella had drunk before, but only on very special occasions like Christmas and birthdays.

Because she was really very hungry, she ate everything that was put in front of her and it was delightful to be sitting in front of a blazing fire.

When the servants who waited on them were not in the room, the Marquis asked her,

"I am interested, Odella, to know why your mother was, as you have told me, so keen for you to speak French."

"She thought it was a mistake for English people to be so insular when they travelled, of course before the war, without taking the trouble to learn the language of the countries they visited."

"I am sure that is true," the Marquis agreed.

"So she had me taught French," Odella went on, "and also Spanish."

The Marquis was about to express his surprise when Odella continued,

"Then, because Papa had no son, and he wanted me to help him with his research, he taught me Latin and Greek. I have always hoped that one day, if I am lucky, I will be able to – go to Greece."

The Marquis was astonished.

Of all the women he knew, practically none of them had had a good education.

He had thought it impossible to discuss foreign countries or their literature, as he enjoyed doing, with anyone but a man.

There were a great many subjects, he thought, that he would have liked to talk about with Odella.

He was very eager, however, to hurry on to London and he was determined to get there in record time.

Wrapped in her warm cloak, Odella climbed into the travelling chariot once again, but now she sat beside the Marquis and she had the fur rug over her legs.

The new team was fresh and they set off at a tremendous pace. It was impossible to talk intimately while they were moving so fast.

They made one more change of horses at another inn.

This time the Marquis reckoned on only a five-minute break before they were off again.

By now the moon was fading, the stars were disappearing and the first ray of the sun was a streak of gold in the East.

It was so lovely that Odella felt as if she was travelling into a magical land where there were no problems ahead but only happiness.

Without being aware of it, she moved a little nearer to the Marquis.

Looking down, he quizzed her,

"You are all right? You are not too tired?"

"I am thinking how – enchanted everything looks," Odella replied,

There was a rapt note in her voice that the Marquis did not miss.

"That is what we will try to make it. We are setting out on a Crusade together to destroy what is evil and to protect what is good."

"That is just – what I want – to do," Odella murmured.

She looked up at him as she spoke.

He knew by the expression in her eyes that she was seeing him as a Knight in Shining Armour going into battle.

'I must protect her from being hurt or disillusioned,' he thought. 'Not only by what we have to do for our country but also from me.'

*

It was eight o'clock in the morning and the sun was now shining in a clear sky.

The Marquis turned his horses into Berkeley Square and stopped outside one of the more impressive houses.

As he did so, a red carpet was rolled across the pavement.

Odella could see waiting there a number of servants in smart livery as well as an elderly butler.

The Marquis helped Odella out of the chariot and they then walked in through the front door together.

"Good morning, my Lord," the butler bowed respectfully. "Your Lordship's orders have arrived about an hour ago."

The Marquis nodded and took Odella up the staircase. Waiting for them at the top was the housekeeper, wearing rustling black silk with a silver chatelaine at her waist.

She curtseyed to the Marquis and he said,

"Good morning, Mrs. Peel. You have prepared a room for Miss Wayne?"

"I have indeed, my Lord."

The housekeeper hurried ahead to open the door of a room along the passage.

As they walked after her, the Marquis said quietly,

"I want you to go to bed and sleep until the afternoon. Remember we will be late tonight and I want you to look your best."

Odella smiled and he went on,

"We will have tea together in the boudoir. Then I will tell you exactly what I have found out."

He lowered his voice as he spoke the last words.

When they reached the room where Mrs. Peel was waiting, he then walked on down the passage.

With difficulty Odella stifled a desire to hang onto him and ask him to stay with her.

But she was already inside the room and Mrs. Peel had closed the door.

"Let me help you to undress, miss," she offered. "The footman will be bringin' up your trunk and, on his Lordship's instructions, your breakfast."

It was much easier, Odella decided, to carry out his Lordship's orders than to think for herself.

She ate the breakfast that had been provided for her and then the climbed into a large and comfortable bed.

Mrs. Peel pulled down the blinds over the windows and drew the curtains to darken the room.

Odella had expected to lie awake thinking over all that had happened, but she fell asleep almost at once.

*

The Marquis went to his own room where his valet was waiting for him.

He also ate a hearty breakfast before he undressed and then he climbed into bed.

"I will sleep for about four hours, Watkins," he said. 'Tell them to have a light luncheon prepared for me then and my phaeton is to be round at two o'clock."

"Very good, my Lord,"

Watkins had been the Marquis's loyal batman when he was in the Duke of Wellington's Army.

He knew by the Marquis's voice and the expression on his face that 'something was up' and he was intensely curious, but he was too well trained to ask any questions.

He knew only that his Master was 'on the warpath'.

He was supremely confident that whatever difficulties may lie ahead that his Lordship would win through.

The Marquis had trained himself during the war to relax completely whenever he had the chance. As it was usually a case of having no more than two or three hours sleep at a time, it was essential that he should not waste the opportunity.

He therefore slept deeply until Watkins called him.

He awoke, aware that what lay ahead of him in the next few hours was vitally important for the future of his country.

And he would need all his wits about him to cope with it all.

He appeared, however, completely at ease when dressed extremely smartly with a high cravat tied in a new and intricate manner as he walked down the stairs.

His phaeton was waiting at the door and he could not resist admiring once again his two new horses that were drawing it.

As he stepped into the driving seat, he said to the butler,

"I hope to be back by four o'clock to have tea with my guest in the boudoir."

"Very good, my Lord," the butler replied.

He bowed as the Marquis drove off, thinking, as he had often thought before, that there was no one in London who could compare with the smartness and good looks of his Master.

The Marquis drove off though the London traffic to Carlton House.

As he entered the courtyard, he saw that the preparations for the evening festivities were already well under way.

The door was then opened by one of the Prince Regent's servants wearing his dark-blue livery.

The Marquis, however, asked not for His Royal Highness but for his secretary, Colonel John McMahon.

"The Colonel is in his room, my Lord," the servant, who had seen the Marquis before, replied, "and his assistant is with him."

"Take me to them," the Marquis ordered.

He knew that Colonel McMahon's assistant was General Sir Tomkins Turner, who had been in the same Regiment as himself in the Peninsular. He thought that he at least would be extremely helpful.

Both the gentlemen were surprised when the Marquis was announced.

Colonel McMahon rose to his feet, saying,

"I am delighted to see you, my Lord. His Royal Highness asked for you yesterday, but was told that you had gone to the country. We were half-afraid that you would not be with us this evening."

"I am certainly coming to the party," the Marquis replied, "but first I have news of grave import to impart to you both."

He shook hands with the General as he spoke and added,

"What I have to tell you must naturally be in the strictest confidence."

The eyes of the two men listening to him widened.

However they understood and Colonel McMahon went to the door of the adjoining room and told his secretary to see that they were not disturbed.

He was also to make sure that there was no one lingering in the corridor outside.

He had known before that, as the servants were always very curious as to what was taking place, they sometimes listened at keyholes.

It was not for any discreditable motive but simply because they wanted to be the first to know what His Royal Highness was likely to do next.

Also, of course, if there was any particularly arduous work for them to do that they had not anticipated.

When the Colonel sat down again, he said to the Marquis,

"Now you can speak without fear of being overheard."

The Marquis told them briefly and in a low voice what had occurred in Portsmouth.

When they learned about the carrier pigeons, the General exclaimed,

"Why did no one think of that?"

"That is what I have been asking myself," the Marquis replied, "but there is more to the story."

He then related what Odella had heard the Frenchman say to the Agent and he was aware that both men stiffened as they listened.

"*Another* attempt!" Colonel McMahon groaned. "How can Bonaparte be so insistent that it is what he wants?"

"He is so desperate," the Marquis answered. "Unless something unforeseen happens, it is only a question of months before the war comes to an end and the death of the Prince Regent would certainly delay or perhaps turn the tide in another direction when it is now flowing firmly in our favour."

"That is true," the Colonel agreed. "What do you want us to do about this assassin?"

"First," the Marquis answered, "I will want to see a list of everyone who has been invited here tonight "

Colonel McMahon rose and, taking a file of papers from a filing cabinet behind him, set it down in front of the Marquis.

The names were all clearly written down in alphabetical order.

The Marquis went through them carefully, looking for foreign names.

The Prince Regent had always been particularly kind to the French *émigrés*, who had come to England during the French Revolution.

Because they heartily disliked the man they called 'that upstart Corsican Corporal', who was ruling France, they had not returned to their country during the Armistice.

At the party the Prince Regent had given in June 1811 to celebrate the inauguration of his Regency, the *émigrés* had been given very special attention and places of honour.

The Marquis had been in Portugal then, but he remembered receiving a letter from his father telling him about the *Grande Fête* at Carlton House.

At the time he had been in a precarious position with his troops on a rugged ledge of the mountains. Also, and it was quite usual in Portugal, there was an acute shortage of food.

The lavishness of the entertainment at Carlton House in London had often tantalised him.

The English from the top downwards had no idea of how the soldiers were suffering in their efforts to beat a tyrant who was determined to conquer Great Britain.

The third Marquis of Midhurst had written to his son,

"The Prince Regent announced on the 19th June that the Fête he had planned to take place at Carlton House would be ostensibly in honour of the exiled Royal Family of France."

Reading the letter, his son thought that this was typical of the Prince Regent and he read on,

"Two thousand invitations were hastily despatched, some to people who are no longer living. When your mother and I arrived, it was to find the bands of the Guards playing in the courtyard and Pall Mall, St. James's Street and Haymarket were blocked with carriages."

He had gone on to describe how the Prince Regent had received his guests in a room hung with blue silk and decorated with gold *fleur-de-lis.*

"All the émigrés were included, the Ducs de Berri, de Bourbon, and d'Angoulême, the Prince de Condé, the Comtes de Lisle and d'Artois, besides Louis XVI's only surviving child, the Duchesse d'Angoulême."

The Marquis had thought when he read the letter that the Prince Regent had certainly done the French of the *ancien régime* proud.

He thought that it was a pity that the French under Napoleon's orders did not appreciate the compliment.

He looked down now at the list of names. Starting with 'A' he found that now, three years later, the Comte d'Artois had been invited and the Duc d'Angoulême.

Under the 'B's there was the Duc de Bourbon and under the 'C's the Prince de Condé.

He continued to work his way down the list.

Then he came upon the Comte Jean de Lisle and he studied the name for a moment before he remarked,

"I may be wrong, but I thought that the Comte de Lisle was dead. I remember my father saying that he was an old man when he talked to him at supper during the *Grande Fête* of 1811."

"Yes, he *is* dead," the Colonel replied, "but I gather that this is a relative."

"Have you met him?" the Marquis enquired.

The Colonel shook his head.

"No, I don't think he has been to Carlton House before, but I believe he is staying as a guest of Mr. Walter Langford and his wife, Lady Georgina, who, you know, is the daughter of the Duke of Cumbria."

The Marquis was silent.

He was thinking intently for a while.

He suddenly recalled that, when he had first paid a visit to Lady Georgina at her house in Bruton Street, she had said,

"Our house is very small, but quite big enough. If one has a large house in Mayfair, one invariably has to have people to stay, not because they wish to see one, but because they want to be in London."

The Marquis knew that this was very true, for he was continually being asked to put up a relative for a few days and, when they arrived, if they were at all popular, he hardly ever saw them.

"I am therefore able to say 'no' to all requests for a free bed," Lady Georgina went on, "except, of course, to some of Walter's friends."

She laughed before she added,

"If he invites someone, he has to give up his dressing room – but he makes them 'pay through the nose' for it!"

The Marquis could well understand that Walter Langford, who was always short of cash, would not give up his dressing room unless he was paid for it.

Now it struck him as strange that the Comte Jean de Lisle would pay to stay with Walter Langford rather than with one of his own relatives.

As he had seen, there were a number of other French friends and relatives coming to the party. Yet perhaps he could not be accommodated by any of them.

He told himself that he was being unduly suspicious and continued down the list.

He found two other French names, Monsieur de Queyrac and the Comte de Valena, on whom he knew that they must keep a strict eye.

He had finished reading the list of names and put the list to one side, when the Colonel enquired,

"Do you intend to speak to His Royal Highness about this?"

"Of course," the Marquis replied. "You know just as well as I do that nothing annoys him more than if plans are made behind his back and he is not in the know, so to speak."

The two men listening to him knew that this was true.

"Very well, come along," the Colonel said. "I will take you to him. But for Heaven's sake make quite certain that he attends to what you have to say. Our job is difficult enough as it is, but at times His Royal Highness seems deliberately to court danger."

The Marquis smiled.

The reason was that the Prince Regent greatly disliked being over-protected and he had been warned several times that the French wished to assassinate him.

He had merely remarked that they would be lucky if they could evade the restrictions he had to put up with at Carlton House.

"Do try your best to make him understand that he really must be careful," the Colonel begged as he led the Marquis along the corridor.

"I will talk to him like a Dutch uncle," the Marquis promised.

However, instead of being amused by this remark, the Colonel looked no less worried.

CHAPTER SEVEN

Odella awoke as Mrs. Peel was pulling back the curtains.

She lay in bed feeling as if she had slept for a very long time like Sleeping Beauty.

Two housemaids carried in a bath, which they set down in front of the fireplace and Mrs. Peel had insisted that they light the fire.

"It's been sunny today," she said, "but now there's a definite nip in the air."

To Odella it was such a delightful luxury to have her bath in front of the fire. It had been scented with the oil of violets, which Mrs. Peel told her came from the Marquis's house in Hampshire.

After her bath she put on one of the simple but pretty muslin gowns that had been packed for her to take to Mrs. Grayson's.

Feeling invigorated she went into the boudoir and the table was already laid in front of the sofa with what she could see was a large and delicious tea.

The only items missing at the moment were the silver teapot and the kettle, which she knew would be brought in when the Marquis arrived.

She thought that the boudoir was a very attractive room and it was decorated with vases of hothouse flowers, which scented the air.

As she looked round, she saw that lying on a stool in front of the fireplace were the daily newspapers.

The sight of *The Times* and *The Morning Post* made her feel guilty.

When her father was at home, he was insistent that she should read the news every day.

"We may live in a small village in what people may think of as 'the back of beyond'," he said, "but we can keep abreast of the situation both here and on the Continent if we read the newspapers regularly."

On his insistence Odella read not only the news but also the editorials every day.

She was aware now that, since her father had left and she had been so involved with the Marquis, she had not looked at a newspaper.

Hastily she picked up *The Morning Post* and read the headlines.

Then, because she was curious about tonight's Reception at Carlton House, she turned to the page that was headed *The Court Circular.*

She thought perhaps that there would be a list of the distinguished people she would see when she arrived there.

She had, however, only just started to read what was printed on that page when the door opened and the Marquis came in.

She could not help giving a little cry of excitement.

He closed the door behind him and came towards her.

"I am back," he smiled, "and I have a great deal to tell you."

"Is – is it good news – or bad?" Odella asked.

Before the Marquis could reply, the butler came in carrying a silver teapot followed by a footman with a kettle.

They placed these down on the large silver tray. Already on it was the tea in a silver box and jugs containing cream and milk besides a sugar bowl.

Odella could not help thinking that it was all very elaborate for two people, but she knew that it was what the Marquis expected.

"Now you pour out the tea," he suggested to her, "and I am quite sure, unless you have had some luncheon, that you are feeling hungry."

"I had a very large breakfast," Odella replied, "and then I slept until less than an hour ago."

'That is exactly what I wanted you to do," the Marquis said. "We are going to have to be very clever this evening, so we will need all our wits about us."

The way he spoke made Odella look at him nervously,

Then, before he could say anything more, the door was flung open and a Vision came into the room.

Staring in surprise, Odella thought that she had never seen anyone look so beautiful and at the same time so flamboyant.

"Michael!" the Vision then exclaimed. "I saw your phaeton driving away from your front door and knew that you had returned."

Lady Georgina seemed to glide across the room towards the Marquis with both hands outstretched.

She was wearing a gown of vivid green satin and her bonnet was decorated with green ostrich feathers that fluttered as she moved.

There were huge emeralds glittering in her ears and she wore an emerald necklace, which flashed with green fire, as did the bracelet that decorated her left wrist.

While the Marquis rose slowly to his feet, Odella could only gasp because she had never before seen anyone looking so fantastic.

"I have only just returned to London," the Marquis informed her without any emotion in his voice.

"And I know that you were coming to see me," Lady Georgina said in a soft caressing voice.

The Marquis perfunctorily raised one of her hands to his lips.

Then he said,

"I am, as it happens, very busy, Georgina."

"But not too busy to see me!" Lady Georgina protested. "How could you be?"

She looked up at him, her head thrown back, her red lips parting provocatively.

The Marquis was suddenly aware that Odella was watching them wide-eyed.

As she glanced in her direction, Lady Georgina said in a very different tone of voice,

"Who is this? And why is she here?"

There was a sharpness in her tone that was unmistakable.

Odella drew in her breath.

"Allow me to introduce Miss Odella Wayne, who is one of my relatives," the Marquis said quietly. "She is coming with me to the party at Carlton House this evening and will be staying here tonight."

"And I suppose she is chaperoned!" Lady Georgina ventured with again that sharp note in her voice.

"Naturally!" the Marquis answered. "You must understand that, as I have a great deal to say to my relatives, who have only just arrived, I must now escort you to your carriage."

It seemed for a moment as if Lady Georgina was going to refuse to leave.

Then, tossing her head and totally ignoring Odella, she walked towards the door while the Marquis followed.

Outside in the corridor she said in a whisper,

"I must see you, Michael. You know how much I have missed you."

"We will talk about it later," the Marquis replied.

Lady Georgina, however, stopped.

"Walter is going away tomorrow."

"Again?" the Marquis exclaimed. "Where is he going this time?"

"To the South Coast on some business of his or other," Lady Georgina said, "so we can be together."

The Marquis did not answer.

He moved towards the stairs and Lady Georgina was obliged to follow him.

As the butler and two footmen were in the hall, they went down in silence.

Only when they had passed through the front door did Lady Georgina stop at the top of the steps.

In a voice that only the Marquis could hear she said,

'Tomorrow night, seven-thirty, and I shall be counting the hours, my dearest wonderful Michael, until then."

The Marquis helped her into her carriage and she waved to him as she drove off, but he made no response.

He was frowning as he walked back into the house.

He knew as he went back up the stairs that Lady Georgina had been a shock to Odella.

He was sure that in the quiet life she had lived in the country she had never seen anyone like her.

Lady Georgina both looked different and also behaved in a manner that was, to say the least of it, indiscreet.

The Marquis was right in thinking that Odella had been shocked.

More than that!

When the Marquis followed behind Lady Georgina from the room, Odella had thought despairingly that this was obviously the woman he loved.

She had, of course, heard when she was in the country of the smart sophisticated ladies of London Society.

But she had never seen one before.

Lady Georgina had therefore been quite a revelation.

As the door closed behind her and the Marquis, Odella had jumped up from the table and run into her bedroom.

She did not understand her feelings, she knew only that she felt upset and distressed.

She was acutely aware of the way Lady Georgina had spoken to the Marquis in that soft caressing voice of hers.

And of the way she had looked at him.

'She loves – him,' Odella told herself.

Then she realised that, of course, he must love her too.

How could he help being fascinated by anyone who was so beautiful and so elegant?

It seemed to Odella that Lady Georgina's eyes had glittered like her emeralds.

'Of – course he – loves her,' she told herself again. 'H-how – could he do – anything else when she is so very – very – beautiful?'

There was a sudden strange pain in her breast.

Because it startled her and was intimidating, she called out aloud,

"Help me – *help me* – Mickie. What do – I do about it?"

Suddenly she was fatefully aware that Mickie was not there – he had somehow become the Marquis.

It was then she realised that, if she had lost the Marquis, she had lost Mickie too.

*

When the Marquis returned to the boudoir, he found it empty and he wondered if he should ask Odella to return to him.

Then he decided that it might make things more awkward than they were already.

There was so much to do this evening and he had no wish to confuse her by talking about Lady Georgina.

Anyway what could he say?

He was perceptive enough to realise that Georgina's behaviour as well as her appearance had undoubtedly shocked the young girl from the country. Even the simplest woman would have been aware that there was a liaison between the two of them.

He helped himself to a cup of tea, hoping that perhaps Odella would come back to the boudoir.

When there was no sign of her, he went downstairs to his study.

He wanted to think very carefully about tonight and of the terrible responsibility he was forcing on Odella.

He was well aware that, if she failed to recognise the Frenchman by his voice and he did attack the Prince Regent, she would feel guilty for the rest of her life.

It was then once again that he had an urgent desire to protect her and to save her, if it was possible, from having to take part in the drama that lay ahead.

She was so young, so unspoilt and so different from any other girl he had ever known.

He could only pray that the evening would not be as terrifying for her as he feared that it might be.

The Colonel said to him confidentially before he left Carlton House,

"This may not be the occasion when the Frenchman attempts to kill His Royal Highness the Prince Regent."

"What do you mean by that?" the Marquis asked.

"There are many other functions taking place this week," the Colonel replied, "and each would give an assailant an opportunity to strike His Royal Highness."

The Marquis thought this was indeed a reasonable argument.

At the same time Odella had heard the Frenchman say that he had the *entrée*.

He knew now that this might mean that he had obtained it through Walter Langford and Lady Georgina.

He could, of course, have questioned her as to why the Comte de Lisle was her guest and staying in her house.

But he he thought that it would be a mistake on his part.

If she repeated what he had said and the Comte was the intending assailant, he would be on his guard.

As he thought further about it, the Marquis told himself that he had never in his life had a more difficult part to play.

He appreciated it that one unwary word could easily change the whole course of events.

If the Frenchman was there that evening, but had decided to wait for a better opportunity, then the Prince Regent could be taken by surprise subsequently.

He walked restlessly about the room.

At last he decided that he would tell Odella as little as possible and the less they talked about it the less frightening it would appear to her.

The Marquis knew that at the Prince Regent's parties, supper was often delayed until the early hours of the morning.

He had therefore ordered a light dinner at seven-thirty and arranged that Odella should be informed.

*

Odella was not aware that the Marquis had returned to the boudoir.

She had stayed in her bedroom and felt as if she had received an unexpected blow on the head and did not know what to do about it.

'How can I be so foolish as to be hurt and upset,' she asked herself, 'because the Marquis loves somebody who belongs to his own world that is so different from mine?'

However, she knew now, if she was honest, that she loved the Marquis.

Then she told herself despairingly that she might just as well love the Man in the Moon.

'When this is over, he will send me back to the country and I will never see him again,' she thought. 'Anyway why should he be interested in me?'

It was something she went on asking herself as Mrs. Peel helped her to dress.

Fortunately the gown that had been packed for the evening with Mrs. Grayson was a very attractive one.

Odella's mother had chosen it as a gown in which she would appear at the first ball to which she was invited.

So it was one in which she was to make a good impression.

It was white, as was expected of a *debutante* and trimmed around the hem with small white roses and green leaves and there were silver ribbons crossing over her breasts, the ends of which cascaded down the back of the gown.

"You looks lovely," Mrs. Peel said in a tone of genuine admiration. "And I've somethin' to put in your hair."

"What is it?" Odella asked her.

"Some white roses exactly the same as those that decorate your skirt," Mrs. Peel replied, "only they're real and they've got ever such a lovely scent."

She pinned them to the back of Odella's golden hair.

Just as she had finished, there was a knock on the door and Mrs. Peel ran across the room to open it.

"Hiss Lordship's compliments," Watkins said, "but he thinks Miss Wayne might like to wear the pearl necklace and bracelet which his mother wore when she was a girl."

Odella heard what was being said.

Then, when the velvet jewel box was brought to her and she opened it, she gave a cry of delight.

The pearls, which were perfectly matched, were threaded with a small diamond between each one. The same applied to the bracelet that Mrs. Peel fastened to her left wrist.

"Now you'll hold your own with any of the ladies that's been invited to Carlton House!" Mrs. Peel exclaimed with satisfaction.

"I doubt that," Odella answered, thinking of Lady Georgina. "But it was very kind of his Lordship and I shall not feel so countrified now that I am wearing this beautiful jewellery."

"There'll be plenty of smart gentlemen ready to tell you what you look like," Mrs. Peel remarked. "I'd be surprised if even His Royal Highness the Prince Regent isn't amongst them!"

Her kind words made Odella feel a little surer of herself.

She went downstairs to where the Marquis was waiting for her in the drawing room.

It was a large exquisitely furnished room.

The chandeliers were all lit and, as Odella came into the room, the Marquis thought that she might be the Spirit of Spring.

She walked towards him and saw that he was not only exceedingly smart but there were decorations on his cut-away evening coat.

As she reached him, she began nervously,

"I-I hope I – look all right – and you will not be – ashamed of me."

"You look very beautiful," the Marquis replied quietly, "and exactly as I wanted you to look."

Odella smiled at him and he felt as if the sun had come out.

"Now, let's go in to dinner," he suggested. "I don't want to be late at Carlton House."

"Is it – going to be a very – big party?" Odella asked him as they sat down at the table in the well-proportioned dining room.

There were many lit candles on the table, which made the diamonds in Odella's necklace glitter.

"Only about one hundred and fifty to two hundred," the Marquis replied. "This is one of His Royal Highness's smaller parties. The larger ones are overwhelming. But they are given in the summer when the Prince Regent can use the lawns, painted terraces and waterfalls of his garden."

"I have read about them," Odella said, "but I never thought that I would be – able to – see them myself."

"And tonight you will see the treasures he has inside the house, which he is continually rearranging."

"Why does he do that?" Odella asked.

"He is always buying new things or producing them from the attics so that they can be displayed for his guests to admire."

Odella laughed.

"It sounds fun!"

"It is for him," the Marquis said, "and you will be able to enjoy them tonight. His friends never know what to expect next."

He made it all sound very light and glamorous.

But when they were in the carriage going towards Carlton House, Odella asked in a low voice,

"You have not – yet told – me what you would expect to happen. How do you – think the Frenchman, if he is there, will try to – kill His Royal Highness?"

"I think," the Marquis said quietly, "that he will use a stiletto as it is easier to conceal about his person."

The Marquis felt Odella sitting beside him give a little shiver and he went on,

"A stiletto is very fine and sharp and, if it passes swiftly into the heart, it is usually a minute or two before the victim succumbs. That gives the assailant enough time to make his get away."

"And – just suppose I don't – remember what his – voice sounds like?" Odella asked in a concerned whisper.

The Marquis reached out and took her hand in his.

"You are not to be nervous," he urged. "Everything we think of, say, do or hear, passes into our brain, which is very like a storage chamber. We can never forget it, nor erase it, nor change it."

"You – mean that – the way that the – Frenchman spoke is recorded in my – brain – and I cannot forget it?"

"It would be impossible for you to do so. It is there and, even if you tell yourself you will never think of it again, it is still in your mind and chronicled for Eternity."

He realised that Odella understood exactly what he was saying as another woman might not have done.

Then she asked him,

"What shall I – do? How shall I tell – you if I – think he is – the man in the – darkened carriage?"

"I have arranged," the Marquis said, "that the Prince Regent will receive his guests in a narrow room that will not be crowded. The only people with him will be his two secretaries, who will both be armed, and the General in charge of the troops that guard him by day and by night."

He paused before he added,

"And, of course, you and I will be there as well."

"Will not – people think that all this is – very strange?" Odella asked.

"I doubt if they will think about it," the Marquis replied, "for the same reason that each guest will be announced individually by one door, walk across the room to where His Royal Highness is standing and then leave by another door, which will lead them back into the main Reception rooms."

"I see what you mean," Odella said slowly.

'His Royal Highness will speak longer to anyone with a French name so that you will have time to hear them answer. If you recognise the voice, do not speak, just touch my arm or my hand as I am standing beside you."

His fingers tightened on hers as he added,

"Now we both have to trust in Fate, or perhaps you would say God, that we don't make any mistakes."

"I have been – praying all – evening," Odella said simply. "I cannot believe that – God would allow that – wicked Bonaparte to win such – a victory."

"That is what we both believe," the Marquis replied, "and I am certain that your prayers will be heard."

He felt Odella's fingers tremble in his and he told himself once again that he would have done anything in his power to save her from having to go through this ordeal.

But he knew that more important than either of them was the fact that Englishmen were still fighting bravely and vigorously against Napoleon.

Although the news from the battlefronts grew more encouraging every day, it would be a mistake to relax until the French were utterly and completely defeated.

The carriage turned into Pall Mall and the Marquis could hear the bands of the Guards Regiments playing in the courtyard of Carlton House.

They were now standing beneath the fine Corinthian portico designed by Henry Holland and the Marquis released Odella's hand seeing that she was looking about her eagerly.

Despite her obvious anxieties she was feeling really excited at seeing Carlton House for the first time.

It had been described by a great number of people as being more impressive than the Palaces in Russia.

They entered the hall with its Ionic columns of brown Siena marble and Odella felt as thrilled as if she was going to one of the children's parties that had been a delight when she was young.

She and the Marquis were then received by members of the Prince Regent's household.

There were several other guests arriving at Carlton House at the same time and Odella was aware that the Marquis had deliberately arranged for them to come to the party early.

She noticed the respect that he was treated with by everyone present.

Next they were taken up to a room on the first floor and she could see at a glance that it was beautifully and expensively furnished.

As they entered the narrow room that the Marquis had described to her, a Major Domo announced the Marquis's name and her own in a stentorian voice.

There was the Prince Regent himself.

He was wearing the uniform of a Field-Marshal and also the glittering Star of the Order of the Garter.

He was now fifty-one years old, but Odella thought that he looked as if he might have been rather older.

He was still handsome although somewhat overblown and extremely fat.

As she curtseyed deeply before him, she realised, as so many other people had done, that his charm was irresistible and his manner was most gracious and courteous.

"I am so delighted to meet you, Miss Wayne," he said, "and my good friend the Marquis has told me how extremely clever you are and how grateful we must all be to you."

Odella blushed.

At the same time she thanked His Royal Highness profusely for what he had said to her.

Her composure and manner, the Marquis now thought, might have been that of a woman twice her age.

"I believe you are interested in pictures," the Prince Regent was saying, "and I hope I may have time this evening to show you some of mine."

"I would like that above everything, Sire," Odella answered, "and I believe your Royal Highness's French furniture exceeds any other collection ever seen in England."

The Prince Regent was clearly delighted at her words of praise.

It always pleased him when people showed a genuine interest in his possessions and he would have gone into a long explanation of exactly how he had obtained the furniture after the French Revolution.

But someone else was announced at that moment by the Major Domo and this meant that the Marquis and Odella had to move to stand on one side of the Prince Regent.

The Colonel and the General stood together on the other side of the room and there were two other gentlemen by the door, ostensibly attendants.

But they had a distinct military air about them and this told Odella that they were His Royal Highness's special guards.

Now the guests were arriving one after another.

After the Prince Regent had said a few words to each of them, they left the room through the opposite door.

Odella had her breath taken away by the ladies' exquisite jewellery and the richness of their gowns. It seemed as if everybody who came to Carlton House was responding to the challenge of the splendour of the house itself.

Odella longed to look at the pictures on the walls and at the furniture, of which there was a great deal in so small a room.

But she knew that she had to concentrate on watching each person as they appeared in the doorway.

As the names were announced, she knew that these could not possibly be the assassin for whom they were looking.

She recognised many of the names because she had read of them in *The Court Circulars* of *The Times* and *The Morning Post.*

There was the Duchess of Devonshire wearing the most fantastic diamonds and then the Duchess of Portland emulated her with sapphires that gleamed in an enormous tiara.

The gentlemen were certainly not to be outdone.

The gold-embroidered coats of the Ambassadors challenged the uniforms of the various Regiments with the Politicians looking rather plain and dowdy beside them even though they wore a number of decorations.

As more and more people filed through, Odella thought excitedly that it was like a scene from an Opera or some event she had read about in a book with her father, but never expected to be actually present when it took place.

She could not help realising that the Prince Regent was very intelligent.

He spoke to all his guests about their interests and lives as if he was really fascinated by them personally.

One he asked about his music, another about the book that he was writing and to a third he spoke of his Racehorses and his stable at Newmarket.

To the ladies he was complimentary, telling one lovely young Duchess that she enhanced his house like a lily. Another he compared with a piece of colourful Dresden china.

The French *émigré* guests, the Duc de Bourbon and the Duc de Berri, succeeded each other.

It was when their names were called out that Odella stiffened and listened intently.

The Comte d'Artois was a very old man, who she knew from the moment he appeared, leaning on a stick, that he was unlikely to be an assassin.

She listened closely to their voices to make totally sure that she recognised the special intonation whenever it came.

Then the Major Domo announced some new guests in his usual stentorian tones,

"Mr. Walter and Lady Georgina Langford, Your Royal Highness, and accompanied by Comte Jean de Lisle!"

The Marquis was standing close to Odella and she was pulsatingly aware of him.

She sensed that he was suddenly alert and she thought that it was because the woman he loved had just walked into the room.

Lady Georgina was looking exceptionally entrancing in a gown of brilliant red silk. It was ornamented round the hem with crimson feathers and also on the shoulders.

She was wearing a ruby and diamond tiara and a necklace of small rubies.

As she moved with a sinuous grace across the floor, her eyes were on the Marquis.

There was an expression in them that made Odella's heart stop beating.

Lady Georgina sank down in a deep curtsey before the Prince Regent and he said to her,

"It is delightful to see you, Lady Georgina, and you are looking even more beautiful than when we last met!"

'Thank you, Sire," Lady Georgina replied. "You always make me feel so happy."

"And that is what you must be tonight," the Prince Regent answered her as he smiled.

Lady Georgina would have spoken to him again, but he turned to her husband.

"Nice to see you again, Langford. Are you backing my horse tomorrow at Ascot?"

"But, of course, Sire," Walter Langford replied. "And how could Your Royal Highness be anything but the winner of that particular race?"

"I only hope you are right," the Prince Regent responded.

The Comte de Lisle had been detained at the door until Lady Georgina and her husband had passed through.

Then, as he came forward, Odella saw that he was a man of well above medium height, not she thought very young and definitely over thirty.

At the same time there was something strong and determined about his face.

The Prince Regent held out his hand.

"I am glad to meet you, Comte," he said. "I have known members of your family for a long time."

"Your Royal Highness is most gracious," the Frenchman replied, "and – "

At the first words he spoke Odella recognised his voice without a shadow of any doubt.

With difficulty she suppressed a cry of horror and put out her hand towards the Marquis.

It was only a slight gesture, but the Frenchman saw it.

With a swiftness that no one expected, he sprang forward.

He flung his left arm round Odella's throat and pulled her back against him.

Then there appeared a long shining stiletto in his right hand and he pressed it against her breast.

"One step towards me," he shouted out in French, "and she dies!"

CHAPTER EIGHT

For a moment everyone seemed paralysed into immobility.

Then the Marquis, looking past the Comte as if giving orders to someone behind him, ordered sharply,

"Don't shoot! I want him taken alive."

The Frenchman instinctively turned his head.

As he did so, the Marquis shot him through the temple.

The explosion from the pistol echoed and re-echoed round the room.

As the Comte staggered backwards, the Marquis then leapt forward and caught hold of Odella.

He picked her up in his arms and without speaking carried her out of the room through the door that the other guests had run through.

He did not, however, go as far as the main Reception room.

As he knew his way round Carlton House well, he turned aside to a room that he thought would be unoccupied.

It was a small anteroom, but elegantly furnished like the rest of the house. There was a profusion of flowers and the candles were lit.

The Marquis pushed the door shut behind him before he set Odella down gently on her feet.

He realised that she was suffering from shock and for the moment he just looked down at her white face.

She was not trembling now, but was very near to fainting.

He pulled her close to him and then very gently his lips found hers.

As he kissed her, he felt her suddenly come alive.

There was a rapture moving within her which was moving within himself as well.

Because he was so afraid that he might have lost her, he kissed her wildly, fiercely and possessively.

Her whole body melted into his and it was just as if they were an indivisible part of each other.

It seemed a long time later before the Marquis raised his head and Odella said in a voice with a lilt in it,

"We – saved him! *We – saved – him!*"

"*You* saved him," the Marquis insisted, "but, my darling, I might have lost you."

His lips then took possession of hers again.

When he finally released her, he thought it quite impossible that any woman could look so ecstatically happy and so unbelievably beautiful.

"I love you!" the Marquis told her in a deep voice. "And I think, my precious darling, that you love me."

"I do – love – you, *I do*!" Odella whispered. "But – I thought – as you loved someone else – you would never – love me."

"I love no one but you," the Marquis asserted, "and I have never been in love as I am now. I knew when that devil threatened to kill you that I could no longer live without you. How soon will you marry me?"

To his surprise Odella looked up at him enquiringly.

"D-did you – really ask me to *marry* – you?" she stammered.

"I want you as my wife, I want you with me always, and never, never again will I allow you to be in such danger as you have just passed through."

"I-I cannot – believe it."

As if she felt shy, she hid her face against his shoulder.

He held her very close and then he said,

"We must be married at once, because I cannot let you out of my sight."

"That – would be – wonderful!" she murmured.

Then, as she looked up at him, her eyes filled with love and she gave a little cry.

"I-I had forgotten – I am – in mourning."

"In mourning?" the Marquis questioned.

"I-I did not – think of it again – but, when I was waiting for – you to come to – tea, I read in the newspaper that my uncle – is dead and that Papa has now come – into the title."

"The title?" the Marquis asked in surprise.

"My uncle's only son was killed early in the war and so Papa now becomes the seventh Earl of Waynehead."

The Marquis was astounded.

He had been completely determined to marry Odella even if she was only the daughter of an obscure, unimportant country Rector.

However it certainly made things much easier as far as his relatives and his own position were concerned that her father should be the Earl of Waynehead.

Odella gave a little sob.

"I – suppose," she said despondently, "we will – have to – wait."

As she spoke, the door opened and the Prince Regent came bursting into the room.

He closed the door behind him and, as he walked towards them, the Earl took his arms from around Odella.

"I have come to thank you, my boy, for saving my life," the Prince Regent addressed the Marquis.

"It was entirely thanks to Odella," the Marquis replied. "She was the only one who could identify him."

"I realise that," the Prince Regent concurred, putting his hand on Odella's shoulder, "and it is difficult to know how I can thank you."

"I am only so thankful, Sire," Odella said, "that I was – able to – recognise the Comte's – voice."

"I can now proceed with my party without any more of this anxiety," the Prince Regent said. "But I do think, Midhurst, that, as I came into the room, you were expressing yourself more eloquently than I am able to do."

"I was asking Odella to marry me," the Marquis replied. "But we have a problem, which I would beg Your Royal Highness with your usual skill to solve for us."

"Of course, of course, I will do my best," the Prince Regent answered gleefully.

The Prince Regent had been unable for many years to take a prominent part in ruling the country.

Because of this, the Marquis knew that he was always delighted when his friends and his Ministers sought his advice on almost any subject.

"Odella has told me, Sire," the Marquis said, "that her uncle, the Earl of Waynehead, has just died and her father has come into the title. She will therefore be in mourning for some months."

The Prince Regent was listening intently and now he responded,

"I saw in today's newspapers that Waynehead had died and, of course, his son was killed some years ago."

"You are always so well informed, Sire," the Marquis smiled.

"As Papa now has some position in Society," Odella murmured, "I suppose I shall have to – wait for at least – six months before I can – be married."

She looked despairingly at the Marquis.

He knew that she was longing to be married no less ardently than he was.

"Well, of course, I have a solution!" the Prince Regent said triumphantly. "You shall be married immediately before anybody connects you with your uncle's death. And, of course, you yourself have been too pre-occupied today to have had time to read the newspapers."

Both the Marquis and Odella stared at him and the Prince Regent carried on,

"The Archbishop of Canterbury is here. He was the next guest to arrive after you left me. I will go now and speak to him. He can marry you in my Chapel tonight and I will, of course, give the bride away."

"Do you really mean that, Sire?" the Marquis enquired.

"Leave everything to me," the Prince Regent replied.

He walked towards the door in a jaunty way that told the Marquis that he was enjoying himself.

Nothing fascinated His Royal Highness more than an intrigue or a special love affair that he could stage-manage and then take the credit when everything turned out right in the end.

As the door closed behind him, the Marquis opened his arms.

Odella ran towards him with the swiftness of a bird in flight.

"Is it – really – possible that – we can be – married – so soon?" she asked breathlessly.

'That is exactly what His Royal Highness is arranging now and all I want to do is to kiss you and tell you how much I love you."

"And – that is just – what I want too," Odella whispered.

It seemed to her as if the Prince Regent had waved a magic wand.

Before anyone in the party was aware that anything unusual was happening, Odella and the Marquis were walking towards the Chapel with the Prince Regent leading the way.

Behind them came his two secretaries, who were the only other people who had been informed.

The Chapel, although small, was well designed.

Under His Royal Highness's direction, several exquisitely carved pews had recently been installed in the Chapel. There were large solid candlesticks that came from an ancient Church and a cross on the altar embellished with precious stones.

The Archbishop of Canterbury was waiting for them at the Altar.

First the Marquis went ahead to stand at the foot of the steps leading to the Altar.

Then the Prince Regent offered Odella his arm.

He walked up the short aisle, moving with the same solemnity that he would have shown had this been Westminster Abbey.

The Marriage Service was a short but moving one.

The Archbishop conducted it with a sincerity that made Odella feel that every word he spoke was part of the Divine and that God was pleased that she and the Marquis were so happy with each other.

As she and the Marquis knelt for the Blessing, she was sure that the angels were singing above them.

As they rose to their feet, the Archbishop said to the Marquis,

"You may kiss the bride."

It was a very gentle kiss, but Odella was aware that the Marquis vowed without words to keep all the promises that he had made at the Altar.

She knew that his heart was hers for all Eternity and that hers was his for the same length of time.

As they walked from the Chapel, the Prince Regent exclaimed,

"Many congratulations, Midhurst, and may I wish you both every happiness. Now I must leave you to attend to my guests."

"But first, Your Royal Highness, I want to thank you," the Marquis said, "for making me the happiest man in the world."

"And me – the happiest woman!" Odella joined in.

The Prince Regent stopped suddenly.

"I was considering while you were being married," he said, "what I could give you as a Wedding present. You have saved my life. Therefore, I think it appropriate, Midhurst, that you should receive a Dukedom. Your wife will certainly be the most beautiful Duchess who any man has ever known."

For a moment the Marquis was too astounded to speak and the Prince Regent went on,

"My personal present to you will be the award of the Order of the Garter. It is what Wellington has already received and I think it only right that you should have it too."

It was impossible for the Marquis to express in words what he wanted to say.

Indeed he went down on one knee and kissed the Prince Regent's hand.

Odella then sank down in a deep curtsey.

"Now," the Prince Regent suggested in a different tone of voice, "let's enjoy ourselves. We will have supper immediately as I wish to drink your health in champagne."

He went ahead when he had finished speaking and the Marquis and Odella followed him.

When they reached the main Reception room, it was to find that it was filled with guests, all chattering excitedly about the drama that had just taken place.

Every trace of the attempted assassination had been swept away.

The only noticeable effect on the guests had been that some of them had to be detained for a short while before they could be presented to His Royal Highness.

The Prince Regent then gave his orders. Instead of waiting as was usual until long after midnight, supper was at once brought to the tables.

They were arranged not only in the dining room but in the magnificent conservatory as well and it was here that Odella found herself sitting on His Royal Highness's right with the Marquis beside her.

On his left was Lady Hertford who he was still enamoured with.

The Marquis would have preferred to keep their marriage secret. But the Prince Regent insisted on telling everybody that it had taken place and, of course, emphasising his own part in their romance.

Odella thought that his reasoning was very logical.

It was that since she had been instrumental in disclosing his assassin, she might now be in danger from other spies who would wish to take their revenge on her.

"The new Marchioness will be safe with her husband, whose war record is known to us all," he related. "And seeing how lovely she is, you will understand that he wants her with him by day and by night."

He said all this in a speech that made all those listening laugh.

Then, while Odella and the Marquis remained seated at the table, everyone including His Royal Highness rose to drink their health.

To Odella it was an unbelievable enchantment that seemed like a dream from another world.

As one delicious course followed another, she had no idea what she was eating.

She knew only that the Marquis was beside her and his vibrations joined with hers.

She felt as if their love encompassed them with a brilliant light that could only come from Heaven.

When supper was finished, the guests were informed that there was gambling in one of the rooms and music in another.

However, because of the drama of the attempt on the Prince Regent's life, it seemed that all they wanted to do was to chatter to one another.

It was then that the Marquis turned to the Prince Regent,

"I feel sure that Your Royal Highness will understand that it is now time for me to take my wife home."

He accentuated the word *wife* and the Prince Regent smiled.

"She is enchanting – absolutely enchanting!" he exclaimed. "Run along, both of you and if you can spare the time, Midhurst, come and see me tomorrow."

"We will do that, Sire," the Marquis replied, "and thank you, thank you from the bottom of my heart."

As Odella rose from her curtsey, the Prince Regent kissed her.

"If your husband looks after you," he said, "mind you look after him. We need men like him in this country not only in war but also when there is peace."

"I promise I will take great care of him, Sire."

They then went from the room, but found it difficult to reach the hall.

So many people wanted to congratulate them.

They also paid so many compliments to the Marquis on his achievements in battle and to Odella on her looks that, when they were about to drive away from Carlton House, she said,

"If we had stayed there any longer, we should become very conceited!"

"There is plenty of excuse for your doing so," the Marquis replied.

Odella laughed.

A servant came with her wrap and put it round her shoulders.

Next another servant then informed the Marquis that his carriage was waiting at the door.

To Odella's surprise the servants and some of the guests pelted them with rose petals.

They hurried into the carriage and, as it drove off, she sighed,

"Now I really feel married. I should have missed all those lovely rose petals if people had not remembered them."

"I can remember only that you are my wife," the Marquis murmured.

As he spoke, he pulled her against him to kiss her.

*

Odella was waiting in the huge four-poster bed for the connecting door into the boudoir to open.

She had not realised before that the Marquis's bedroom was on the other side of it and she thought now that he had deliberately put her there so that she could be near to him.

She gave just a fleeting thought to the unhappiness and misery that she had felt when she had believed that he was in love with Lady Georgina.

But because she was so aware of his feelings, she knew that after tonight he would never want to think about Lady Georgina again.

Whether or not she had known that the Frenchman staying in her house was a would-be assassin, she and her husband had been instrumental in bringing him to Carlton House where he would murder His Royal Highness with his evil stiletto.

Odella did not know much about the Social world.

Yet she had the idea that, without saying anything, the ladies would draw their skirts to one side when Lady Georgina appeared.

Invitations to balls and parties would no longer be forthcoming for her and she would take no part in them as she had before.

Whatever the Marquis might have thought about Lady Georgina in the past, Odella knew now that it was she he loved.

There was no reason now for her to be jealous of anybody.

'He loves – me! *He – loves me*!' she whispered to herself.

Even as she did so, the communicating door opened.

The Marquis then came into the room and, because she was so excited to see him, Odella flung out her arms.

He sat down on the side of the bed and, taking her hands in his, he kissed first one and then the other.

"How is it possible," he asked, "that you can be so lovely and at the same time so clever? And now you are mine!"

"That is – what I want – to be," Odella murmured.

"You *are* mine," the Marquis was insistent, "and you will never be afraid again or risk your precious self in any wild drama in which you should not have been involved in the first place."

"It was an adventure, a Crusade and we won the final victory!" Odella pointed out.

She then thought that the Marquis was going to kiss her.

Instead he took off his robe and climbed into the bed.

He then pulled her gently against him and sighed,

"My darling, my sweet, I love you with my heart, my soul and also with my body. But I am afraid of hurting or frightening you."

Odella gave a little laugh that was like the song of the birds.

"How could you ever frighten me," she asked, "when I know that our love is perfect and Divine? When you kiss me – I feel I am – touching the stars."

It was then that the Marquis kissed her.

He knew that she had spoken the truth.

He could feel the ecstasy that she was experiencing seeping through her.

It communicated itself to him until they were flying together in the sky.

It was an unbelievable rapture that he had never known before.

When he made Odella his, they touched the peaks of ecstasy.

Then they were enveloped with the Spirit of Love, which comes from God and exists in a Heaven made specially for lovers.

OTHER BOOKS IN THIS SERIES

The Barbara Cartland Eternal Collection is the unique opportunity to collect all five hundred of the timeless beautiful romantic novels written by the world's most celebrated and enduring romantic author.

Named the Eternal Collection because Barbara's inspiring stories of pure love, just the same as love itself, the books will be published on the internet at the rate of four titles per month until all five hundred are available.

The Eternal Collection, classic pure romance available worldwide for all time.